# THE LOST ART OF
# ENOCHIAN
## MAGIC

# THE LOST ART OF ENOCHIAN MAGIC

## Angels, Invocations, and the Secrets Revealed to Dr. John Dee

John DeSalvo, Ph.D.

Destiny Books
Rochester, Vermont • Toronto, Canada

Destiny Books
One Park Street
Rochester, Vermont 05767
www.DestinyBooks.com

Destiny Books is a division of Inner Traditions International

**Library of Congress Cataloging-in-Publication Data**
DeSalvo, John A.
  The lost art of Enochian magic : angels, invocations, and the secrets revealed to
Dr. John Dee / John DeSalvo.
     p. cm.
  Summary: "A practical guide to Dr. John Dee's angelic magic"—Provided by
publisher.
  Includes bibliographical references (p.        ) and index.
  ISBN 978-1-59477-344-0 (pbk.)
  1. Enochian magic. 2.  Dee, John, 1527–1608.  I. Title.
  BF1623.E55D47 2010
  133.4'3—dc22

                                                                                    2010000829

Printed and bound in the United States by Lake Book Manufacturing

10 9 8 7 6 5

Text design by Jon Desautels and layout by Priscilla Baker
This book was typeset in Garamond Premier Pro with Bodega Sans, Helios, and
Gill Sans used as display typefaces

Excerpts from *John Dee's Five Books of Mystery* by Joseph Peterson, copyright 2003
by Red Wheel/Weiser LLC, are reproduced with permission.

To send correspondence to the author of this book, mail a first-class letter to the
author c/o Inner Traditions • Bear & Company, One Park Street, Rochester, VT
05767, and we will forward the communication, or contact the author directly at
**drjohn@gizapyramid.com** or **www.myangelmagic.com**.

*I would like to dedicate this book to my parents,*
*John and Nina DeSalvo.*
*If it wasn't for their encouragement, love,*
*and cultivation of my spiritual curiosity,*
*this book would never have been written.*
*I also dedicate it to my wonderful and supportive family:*
*my wife, Valerie, and my children,*
*Christopher, Stephen, Paul, and Veronica.*

# CONTENTS

*O Lord, I humbly ask you to send me the help of some pious and wise philosopher to help me understand spiritual truths. And if there is no man like this now living on earth, than I beseech your Divine Majesty to send me from the heavenly realm your good and holy spiritual ministers and angels, like Michael, Gabriel, Raphael, and Uriel, or any other true and faithful angels of your choosing who may teach me both natural and supernatural knowledge.*

PRAYER (PARAPHRASED) OF
DR. JOHN DEE (1527–1608)

*God cannot know himself without me.*

MEISTER ECKHART (1260–1328)

*The organized religions and the new age techniques that I've been involved in for decades don't give me the experience of the presence of God which I was searching for. They were just more ideas and theories about God. I don't want more talk, sermons, useless techniques, or rituals. What I want in my life is to experience the peace, love, and presence of God right now. I don't want to spend years developing a new method, spend a lot of money in classes, or have to join organizations and groups. I want to be able to touch God and feel his presence in a natural and easy way. I want to experience God's Magic.*

A SEEKER OF GOD

# FOREWORD
## By Lon Milo DuQuette

I was gratified beyond words when John DeSalvo asked me to pen a few words for his marvelous work. I can say without hesitation that the reader is in for an exciting, provocative, and enlightening experience; for some of you it may also be the beginning of an adventurous journey of self-discovery.

This is a work that I believe could only have been written in the morning hours of the twenty-first century, when advanced scientific thought is promising us an unprecedented understanding of the cosmos and the nature of matter and energy. As our astro and quantum physicists draw closer to the Holy Grail of a theory to explain it all, can it be possible that we're approaching a level of inquiry so profound that we will soon be required to dramatically expand our level of consciousness in order to process the multidimensional answers?

I believe the answer is "Yes," and as we penetrate ever deeper into these new frontiers of thought, we're confronted with the same fundamental issues and challenges that have faced *spiritual* scientists since the dawn of human consciousness: How was the universe created? How can it be limitless? What sustains it? Will it ever end—if so, how? What is the nature of time, space, reality, and consciousness? Who and what am I? When the musings of Science soar to these heights, and try as it might to do otherwise, Science is forced by the limitations of word-images to evoke the metaphoric language of mythology, mysticism, and magic in her attempt to even *discuss* these transcendent matters.

Why, then, should it be thought "unscientific" for us to explore these same issues directly by magical means? After all, for tens of thousands of years of human history, right up until the eighteenth century, magic *was* science. Magic* is the mother of mathematics, astronomy, biology, chemistry, architecture, and medicine. It does no good to argue that mythology, mysticism, and magic are irrational and illogical, for indeed, the mysteries of astrophysics and quantum mechanics appear to be so as well.

For the better part of a thousand years, adepts of the Holy Kabbalah† have, by means of a variety of curious techniques, endeavored to use the mind to transcend the mind. For the sake of convenience, they view "God" as the absolute and supreme consciousness of the universe, and individual humans as miniature reflections of the supreme consciousness—"Man made in the image of God." Just as my reflection in the bathroom mirror "lives" only because of my living presence, so too do I exist as a reflected unit of the supreme consciousness. My seeming separation from God is as illusionary a phenomenon as my reflection in the mirror; mistakenly I believe that my reflection is real and somehow estranged from the physical me.

Because God and humans are two aspects of the same consciousness, the Kabbalists view us both as being divided (categorized would be a better word) into four main levels of consciousness:

- The lowest level (as an aspect of the supreme consciousness) is the *material plane* itself. Specific example: a rocking chair. For us (as an aspect of the individual consciousness) this level manifests as our physical bodies.

---

*"Magic" (a spiritual art) is sometimes spelled "magick" to distinguish it from the acts of a stage magician. It's interesting that many attribute the variant spelling of *magick* to Aleister Crowley. In fact, the variant spelling occurred in the first English translation of Cornelius Agrippa's *Occult Philosophy* in 1651.
†The Kabbalah is Judaism's esoteric science of the soul. The word itself is based upon the three Hebrew letters of Kof [ ק ], Bet [ ב ], and Lamed [ ל ] and is often rendered as "Qabalah," "Qabala," "Cabala," "Kabalah," or "Kabbalah."

- The next level (as an aspect of the supreme consciousness) is the *formative plane* where the patterns of everything that will manifest on the material plane exist. Specific example: the idea or concept of a rocking chair. The Kabbalists call this the world of angels. For us (as an aspect of the individual consciousness) this level is our intellect—our mind's eye.

- Above this (as an aspect of the supreme consciousness) is the *creative plane* where the great general principles of the universe are generated. Specific example: the concept of sitting down. The Kabbalists call this the world of archangels. For us (as an aspect of the individual consciousness) this level manifests as mysterious powers of intuition. An example of this would be when a mother awakes in the night when her child has been in an accident far away—an ability that transcends logic, time, and space.

- Above this (as an aspect of the supreme consciousness) is the *archetypal plane*. For all intents and purposes we could consider this the consciousness of the godhead itself. Specific example: the universal concept of rest. For us (as an aspect of the individual consciousness) it's the life force itself—ultimately our true identity.

In the metaphoric language of Hebrew mysticism, the mechanics of creation and the cooperative symphony of all the natural forces of the cosmos are a well-ordered hierarchy of spiritual agencies—archangels, angels, spirits, and demons. We also have our special place in this hierarchy, and a special duty to perform. As humans, living on the material plane, we're the culmination of the process. We resonate with a full collection of the echoes of the entire creational cycle. Each of us, as a monad of the supreme consciousness, is a tuning fork vibrating as the pure *lower harmonic* of the absolute *note*.

It's the job (indeed, I believe it's the destiny) of each of us to raise our consciousness step by step, octave by octave, back up to the godhead. This is the true initiatory adventure each of us is destined to undergo. This is the Great Work.

One branch of Kabbalistic philosophy views the cycle of the descent into matter and the return journey home as a *ten-step* process; the roadmap being a schematic diagram called the *Tree of Life*. The Enochian vision magic of Dr. John Dee, however, divides the trip not into ten levels, but *thirty*, and it's the step-by-step exploration of these thirty Aethyrs or heavens of human/divine consciousness that's the fascinating subject of Dr. DeSalvo's bold and visionary experiences.

As I don't wish to delay your reading adventure one moment longer, I shall now close this little contribution to my friend's wonderful book. But before I do, I would like to leave you with something to think about as you ponder the implications of your own journey back to the supreme consciousness. It's called *The Secret of the Shem-ha Mephorash* (the sacred seventy-two-part "divided" name of God), and it is from the Epilogue of my book *The Chicken Qabalah of Rabbi Lamed Ben Clifford*.

### The Secret of the Shem-ha Mephorash[1]

*God is.*

*Undivided God is pure potentiality and realizes*
*Nothing.*

*God can only realize Itself by becoming Many and then*
*experiencing all possibilities through the adventures*
*of Its many parts.*

*The ultimate purpose for My existence is to exhaust My*
*individual potentiality.*

*My Love of God and God's love of Me springs from the*
*Great Secret we share.*

*The Secret is—*

*God and I will achieve Supreme Enlightenment at the*
*same moment.*

---

Lon Milo DuQuette (Rabbi Lamed Ben Clifford) is an American writer, lecturer, and occultist. He has written several successful books on Western mystical traditions including *Angels, Demons & Gods of the New Millennium, Enochian Vision Magick,* and *Tarot of Ceremonial Magick.* He is perhaps best known for his autobiography, *My Life with the Spirits,* which is currently a required text for two classes at DePaul University in Chicago. Many of DuQuette's books have been dedicated to analyzing and exploring the works of Aleister Crowley (1875–1947), the English occultist, poet, and philosopher. DuQuette occasionally appears on radio and television as a guest expert on subjects involving the occult. He is on the faculty of the Omega Institute in Rhinebeck, New York, where he teaches a seminar on the Western magical tradition.

# ACKNOWLEDGMENTS

I'm extremely grateful to my very good friend and colleague Lon Milo DuQuette, whose book *Enochian Vision Magick: An Introduction and Practical Guide to the Magick of Dr. John Dee and Edward Kelley* first inspired me to enter the world of angelic magic. I am extremely honored that Lon agreed to write the foreword to this book and am most appreciative of his constant guidance, encouragement, and most importantly, his friendship.

I want to thank my wonderful wife, Valerie, for the amount of time and effort she spent in proofing the entire manuscript and for her invaluable suggestions and comments. I have very much appreciated her loving encouragement while I was writing this book. No husband could ask for a more supportive wife.

Warm thanks to Joanne St. George for her unwavering support and love throughout my entire life. Her excitement for all my projects has kept me going. Joanne has a true love of God and her fellow human beings; there are few people in the world like her.

I'm immeasurably indebted to my very close friends Marty and Judy Stuart for their constant help, suggestions, and encouragement throughout the writing of this book. I especially want to thank Judy for reading the entire manuscript and for her editorial recommendations, which have been invaluable. Marty and Judy have guided me through all the ups and downs of this project and are the dearest people in the world. May God bless them as they have blessed so many others with their spiritual gifts.

I'm also extremely grateful to one of my closest friends and colleagues, Becky Andreasson, for all of her help and guidance. She made wonderful suggestions regarding the organization of the chapters in the book and its content. Becky's unique spiritual insights and gifts have blessed me through our many years of friendship.

Warm thanks to Betty Andreasson, whose friendship and encouragement have also been a tremendous help to me. I am most grateful to her for her friendship and extensive knowledge of many areas of biblical research.

J. J. Hurtak, Ph.D., has been my very good friend and colleague for many years, and I want to thank him for his suggestions on streamlining the Enochian Meditation and recommending specific psalms to use. He has been a source of constant support and encouragement to me.

Desiree Hurtak, Ph.D., has also given me continued support and encouragement throughout the many years of our friendship. She is a person with truly unique gifts and insights.

I'm indebted as well to the late Nick Nocerino, who was the world's foremost expert on crystal skulls. Nick was a true friend, and I miss him very much.

I would like to thank my very good friend David Salmon for many hours of discussion and brainstorming sessions. He has been an invaluable help on all my books, and I'm grateful for his advice. David is one of the most knowledgeable people I've ever met.

Joseph Peterson explained to me the organization and makeup of the tables in the Book of Enoch, especially the first leaf. I'm also very grateful to him for permission to quote from his most excellent and valuable book, *John Dee's Five Books of Mystery*. I have enjoyed many hours of stimulating conversation with this most brilliant researcher and scholar.

Jeremy Kay, a good friend, helped me with background information for the practice of ritual magic. He is still just as creative as when he was the art director for the movie *Easy Rider*. I enjoyed our many hours of conversation and offer him my sincere thanks for all of his great help.

To two of my closest and dearest friends, Dan and Nancy Schmidt, who told me of my interesting connections with Dr. John Dee and who have given me the best advice on how to write, my sincere gratitude. As well, Dan is one of the most knowledgeable people in almost every area of metaphysics and has generously supplied me with much source information.

I very much appreciate my very good friend and colleague Paul Maloney for his discussions and suggestions regarding ancient artifacts. I've enjoyed many hours of conversations with Paul; I always learn something new from our discussions.

I also want to thank the staff of the many public libraries across the nation and throughout the world for their help and access to many rare books and manuscripts. I especially want to thank the British Library for permission to use the photographs of me holding copies of the diaries of Dr. John Dee and for preserving and maintaining the original Dee manuscripts.

There are very few people in the world that one is eternally grateful to, but Jon Graham is one of those people in my life. He has been responsible for seeing that my most important spiritual books have been published. It's my belief that these books are capable of helping many people on their spiritual path. My deepest appreciation and thanks go to him.

I'm indebted and grateful to my wonderful, creative, and talented editor, Anne Dillon. No author could have a better editor. This is Anne's second book with me, and I'm very thankful for all she has done.

I would like to thank the following booksellers and friends for supplying me with important books and research information: Sasha Pasich of Motusbooks, Michael Cottingham of Voyage Botanica, and Richard Vokoun of Rain Dog Books.

And last but not least, warm thanks to my son Paul for his help with the photographs in this book and his wonderful lunches, which kept me going during my many periods of intense writing.

# INTRODUCTION

Initially I was planning to write a book about the history of magic and how its most important phase and development occurred during the Renaissance. This was the age of magic, and almost all kinds of ritual magic that exist today are based on the works of Renaissance magicians such as Henry Cornelius Agrippa, Dr. John Dee, Albertus Magnus, Johannes Trithemius, and several others. However, the more I researched Renaissance magic and the works of these magicians, the more I realized that the basis or foundation of magic is the Enochian Magic, which was communicated to Dr. John Dee by the angels in the sixteenth century. In fact, the angels told Dee that this was the same knowledge and wisdom that Enoch of the Bible had been given by the angels.

It appears that this Enochian Magic is the most powerful form of magic known to humans.

Readers are always curious about the personal beliefs and spiritual experiences of authors of metaphysical books such as this one. They are interested in knowing whether or not the authors are merely scholars who research and write about occult phenomena or whether they have actually practiced or experienced what they have written about. Questions are likely to be along the lines of: Do the authors really believe in the metaphysical or spiritual phenomena that they are writing about, or are they skeptics? Have they experienced or attempted to do any of the practices and rituals they discuss? Have they seen or communicated with angels, demons, or spirits and entered high spiritual realms in order to experience these worlds? I'm sure that many more questions may occur to the reader, and I believe that all of them are legitimate. Given this, I will share with you some of my own personal beliefs and experiences as they relate to Enochian Magic and its practice.

I believe in one God who is infinite in all aspects (power, knowledge, and bliss) and is a loving and just God who created everything—both the physical and spiritual realms. I believe that all humans have a part of the spirit of God within them, and this spirit never dies but eventually returns to its original source (which is also God). Our spirit will always have an independent existence and consciousness. Our goal as individuals is to perfect ourselves until we form the complete likeness of God.

There is a very old Sufi saying that *there are as many paths to God as souls in the world,* and I truly believe this. We will be learning about the many paths to God by studying these lost Enochian teachings, which are so necessary for humanity today when so much confusion and fear abound. Deep down, we all have a longing to find out who we are, where we came from, where we're going, and what the purpose of our life is. I find this hunger in almost everyone I meet, but many people have sublimated this urge in favor of an unbalanced way of life, which focuses on the acquisition of material things at the expense of developing an inner spiritual life.

I believe in the absolute reality of the spiritual worlds and realms, which are comprised of spiritual creatures, including angels and demons. Magic is concerned with harnessing and using these unseen energies to change events and outcomes in our physical world. We're humans composed of a physical body and a spiritual body. Magic can affect both types of bodies. We enter the magical world through our magical or spiritual senses. We're all born with these spiritual senses, but they lay dormant in us and must be awakened and developed. Just like an infant learning how to see and hear, we need to relearn how to use these senses.

I believe that magic's real purpose isn't to ask for things and manipulate the angels and demons to do our bidding but to use magic as a meditation that will enable us to come into the presence of God.

Magic isn't as alien to most of us as we would like to think. We don't realize, for instance, to what extent magic has penetrated our everyday lives. For example, the rituals in many of our churches are loaded with remnants of ancient magical rites and rituals. I've practiced many forms and types of magic but only have had significant results with Enochian Magic; it's currently the only type of magic I practice. In my studies and experiments, I've come to the conclusion that this magic is important for every person to know and be able to practice. This book will teach you how to practice this magic.

One of the most important features of this book is the instructions for carrying out your own magical ritual, which I've called the Enochian Meditation (EM). In any type of magic, the magician or magus makes sure that he or she is protected in a magical circle so that he or she cannot be harmed by any spirits, angels, or demons. Most practitioners use the Lesser Banishing Ritual of the Pentagram (LBRP), which I will also teach you. This rite is performed before and after all magical ceremonies and rituals. It's a simple procedure and only takes a few minutes to do. It can also be used like a meditation to clear and purify the spiritual atmosphere around you.

Not only can magicians conjure angels or demons* to carry out their will and requests, but they can also prevail upon them in order to gain knowledge and wisdom, both of the present and the future. This is what motivated Dr. John Dee in the sixteenth century to engage in angelic communications. He was seeking the spiritual knowledge and wisdom that he felt he could only get from the otherworldly realm of the angels.

These otherworldly realms are not in your imagination or in the

---

*In general, when the term *invocation* is used, it means summoning the good angels. The term *evocation* usually means summoning evil angels or demons (many authors use these terms interchangeably). Although I will be discussing this in general, I will not be teaching you the evocative type of magic.

mind but are real and have an independent existence. These realms would remain present even if our present physical realm were completely destroyed; they don't depend on us for existence. In fact, it's the other way around. We're, in a sense, shadows of them, and their world is more real than ours. We are a reflection of the higher spiritual realms.

I believe magic and invoking angels are the oldest spiritual practices of human beings, and they survived to this day because they are very real and effective practices. When magic is suppressed, like in times past by the church or state, it survives underground, and a small group is given the responsibility of preserving it for the whole of humankind.

It has only been in the last few centuries that magic has been viewed as a superstitious practice. But I believe magic is scientific and follows a higher scientific law. In this book, for the first time ever, I present my theory on the scientific basis of magic. I think this will shed much light on an important mechanism of how and why magic works. Much of my hypothesis is based on a recognition of a neurological process whereby sound resonates and triggers specific reactions in our brain and nervous system, opening us up to higher dimensions, worlds, and their inhabitants. In this case, the sound that I'm referring to takes the form of Enochian Calls, or specific syllables that are pronounced out loud as invocations. (I will elaborate on these Enochian Calls later in the book.)

Since the time of Dr. Dee, it has been difficult for many interested scholars to determine exactly how the angels wanted the Enochian Calls pronounced. These Calls are the key to Enochian Magic. From 1583 to 1587, Dee received the Angelic Calls directly from the angels, and he wrote them down in his diaries. (These diaries were first typeset and published by Meric Casaubon, D.D., in 1659, many years after Dee's death in 1609.)

Casaubon did his best to transcribe Dee's poor handwriting and Early English spelling into something that could be printed, and for the most part, he did a good job. The majority of books to date on the subject have reprinted the Calls from Meric Casaubon's publication. I, however, have researched the British Library's original scans of Dee's manuscripts to arrive at what I believe are the correct pronunciations of these calls.

I hope my book will help each individual on his or her spiritual search or path. I believe that this is the goal of life, and if we can determine God's original purpose for us, it will help us progress in the right direction toward him. My wish for you is that *The Lost Art of Enochian Magic* will bring you closer to God and help you to experience his presence in a very real and transformative way.

# 1

# MAGIC AND ITS INFLUENCE ON OUR EVERYDAY LIVES

Today, when many people hear the word *magic,* they think of stage magic, such as magic tricks performed using sleight of hand, or something evil and dark—magical rituals carried out by black-clad individuals chanting strange-sounding words and using all manner of magical implements, including wands, daggers, incense, and candles.

Numerous occult movies have contributed greatly to these misconceptions. Maybe this is what magic has become, but is this what magic was in the beginning and what it was really meant to be? I believe the answer is no.

## What Is Magic?

My definition of magic is that it's a ritual or meditation that enables individuals to move along their spiritual path toward God. It's the goal of all humans to find God and to be present with him. Magic is a gradual process and a development of one's spiritual nature to become attuned to God. This movement toward God will continue to build in strength until the goal of reaching cosmic consciousness and oneness with God is finally attained in its fullest expression.

But how can magic do this? And what is magic, really?

Magic has been with us collectively since time immemorial and with us individually since childhood. Most of us grew up with stories of magic. For my generation, it was depicted in fables, such as *The Arabian Nights*. For today's generation, it's depicted in tales, such as *The Lord of the Rings, Star Wars,* and *Harry Potter,* as well as in numerous television shows, books, and even music. We're all exposed to the theme of magic on a daily basis. Maybe, as a child you wondered, as I did, whether or not magic was real and what it really was.

I don't believe there is a simple definition of magic, but it *can* be described. In getting to that, first I would like to focus on our physical reality and what it's comprised of. Our physical reality is made up of matter and energy, which obey the laws of physics, thermodynamics, and the conservation of matter and energy. Our physical world, or our reality, consists of the earth, the solar system, the entire universe, and whatever we can feel, touch, hear, see, and measure (including black holes, nebulas, and dark matter) with scientific instruments. Our physical world even consists of energies that we cannot measure.

We must assume that there are other realities or dimensions or spiritual planes that exist in addition to our physical world. What are these other realities? Since they don't behave like physical objects and follow our known scientific laws, it's more difficult to describe them. These other realities, dimensions, and realms are actually higher spiritual realities or dimensions—our physical world is but a lower shadow of a higher spiritual reality. There are many spiritual realms, one higher than the next. Where do they end? And where do they begin?

Picture a flat piece of paper with a square in the middle. This square, which has four sides, represents our physical world. Many spiritual traditions agree that four is a number that symbolizes the earth. There are four directions (north, south, east, and west), four elements (fire, air, earth, and water), and four winds, for example. Now picture a circle surrounding this square. This first circle is the first spiritual realm. Then draw another circle around this one. This is the next, higher spiritual realm. Continue drawing until you have thirty circles. These are the thirty Aethyrs or spiritual realms, which we will be discussing later in this book and using magic to enter.

At the very top is God; we're at the very bottom. God is the First Cause or Light, Love, or the Force (whatever you want to call him). God created the universe by a word or a sound (Om Point or Word of God). The syllable OM was considered by Indian sages to be a sacred sound that was uttered by God and its vibration caused the creation of all things. It is a powerful mantra that is used in Eastern meditation. The first created realm may be called the highest heaven or realm of the Holy Spirit, and it's just below God. The next spiritual realm, which is a *reflection* of the highest plane but a step lower, is the realm of the archangels. The plane below this one is the plane of the lower angels. We continue on down through these planes, all thirty of them, until we reach the plane of the physical world where we are; this is the lowest reflection of all of the previous planes.

Please bear in mind that these planes or realms are all interconnected and inside one another, but one is higher than the next in terms of its spiritual dimension. Also, each of these realms or planes, like our physical world, is real and is composed of its own substances and beings—its own angels or governors, as they are called, that control and monitor their particular world. These angels will also be our guides when we enter these spheres. As we move up through the spiritual realms or Aethyrs, we're all the time moving closer to God and experiencing his presence more and more.

Besides experiencing the different realms and obtaining knowledge and wisdom through the use of magic, it's possible to work with the angels in order to cause a desired change in the physical realm. But we have to be careful here because this is where we must distinguish between white and black magic, or between good and evil. Manipulating the angels in these higher planes for good is considered white magic; using them for evil or selfish purposes is considered black magic. To my mind, it's not advisable to use the angels for any purpose other than to find God.

Many books have been written about finding God, but unless you can experience this fully realized mystical union for yourself, it's all just theory. And God doesn't want us to theorize about him, he wants us to *experience* him. Many other techniques to find God have been developed, but some require years of practice and exercise, costly classes and instruction, and are difficult for the average person to undertake. That's why he gave magic to the first humans, who have passed it down from one generation to the next since the beginning of time.

According to ancient Jewish tradition, certain mystical and metaphysical teachings were given to man by the angels. This is mentioned in several Kabbalist texts, which claim that the angel Raziel gave these mystical teachings to Adam to restore his communion and relationship with God after the Fall. It's also the same knowledge that Enoch, a prophet in the Old Testament, was given by God. It may also be the same information that Solomon was given when God asked him what he wanted and Solomon responded by asking for wisdom, not riches or fame.

As stated in the introduction, from time to time this magic was lost to humankind. When this happened, the angels attempted to restore it. Its most recent appearance was in the sixteenth century, when the angels restored it to humankind by transmitting it to Dr. John Dee of England, one of the most famous mathematicians and scholars of his day.

## Magic and the Church

Magic and occult practices, designed to allow us to become closer to God, have been considered by some people to be against the teachings of the Bible, organized religion, and church tradition. This belief has been perpetrated since at least the Middle Ages, when the Church was afraid of losing its power over and control of the people. The perceived threat, which magic represented, was that it advocated a spiritual technique whereby a person could make spiritual progress and even be in the presence of God and the angels directly, without the help of a priest or church. How blasphemous was that!

The problem remains with us. Churches today are dependent on their parishioners for survival; it's a big business. If someone could get spiritual help—and get it more efficiently without the intervention of an ordained minister, priest, bishop, or pope—this would really threaten organized religion. It's all about control and power, and of course, it's ultimately about money. I'm not saying that all churches, ministers, and priests are power hungry, but the system perpetuates itself. There are many sincere and honest churchgoers who think they have no place to turn for spiritual direction but to the church. So you can see how the early Church perceived the practice of ritual magic as one of the biggest threats to its survival.

Ironically enough, the Catholic mass in a sense resembles a magic ritual and even uses magical words. When Catholics attend mass, they witness the priest doing something that involves a mystical ceremony using mystical words. This occurs during the part of mass that we call the Consecration, when the priest says specific words over ordinary bread and wine. The Church claims and believes that during this ritual, the bread and wine have been changed into the body and blood of Jesus Christ. The Catholic Church believes that this change, which it calls transubstantiation, really occurs—and isn't just symbolic, as many Protestant faiths believe. Catholics also claim that although we still see only the bread and the wine, it really has been changed to the body and blood of Jesus even though we're not able to perceive the change on a physical level.

It's important to note that the priest must use specific words for the transformation to occur. (In a magic ritual, specific words must also be used.) Another thing to realize is that not just anyone can invoke the actual transubstantiation—one must be an ordained Catholic priest. To become an ordained priest, a special ceremony is held wherein a bishop who has specific powers says certain words over the priest to confer this power to him.

Another interesting ritual in the Catholic Church is the Exposition of the Blessed Sacrament, in which a host is put in a monstrance (vessel) and displayed on the altar. The faithful pray in front of it. This is akin to a ritual that the Egyptians performed, and in fact, if you compare these rituals side by side, they appear to be very similar. (See plate 3 of the color insert.)

Today, there is stagnation in religion, in its rites and practices. Modern religion has lost its thrust and its ability to inspire; it doesn't encourage true spiritual growth. That's why so many people, especially the young, are disaffected and are leaving churches in droves. Just as the practices of organized religion have deteriorated, so too have the practices of magic exercised by many occult groups today. Some individuals in the nineteenth century tried to apply the Enochian Magic of Dr. Dee and use it in their own magic societies. I believe they didn't do this correctly, and Dr. Dee's magic was added to their own beliefs and philosophy and thereby corrupted.

In this book, we will explore the path that magic offers us to reclaim our spirituality and bring us closer to God. Not only will we survey ancient and modern magical practices, we will show that these practices were natural and accepted elements of religious life in ancient times and were even part and parcel of the lives of the biblical patriarchs. In the first few centuries, many early Christians practiced magic as well.

## Enochian Magic Resurfaces in the Renaissance

Before we get into a more detailed discussion of Enochian Magic, it would be useful to have some additional background information on the history of magic. As stated earlier, I believe that when Enochian Magic was lost through the years, the angels restored it to human beings, most recently during the Renaissance when Dr. John Dee communicated with the angels to obtain it.

Please keep in mind that Dee was no fool. He was an extremely accomplished scientist, mathematician, and scholar, as well as being a very sincere spiritual pilgrim. He was an advisor to Queen Elizabeth and to many famous explorers of the time. John Dee had one of the largest libraries in the world, which included some of the rarest occult and metaphysical books in existence. Many were one-of-a-kind manuscripts.

I believe that John Dee was the instrument of God to bring the technique of Enochian Magic to the world. He sincerely believed it, too. He also believed that the Prophet Enoch, mentioned in the Bible (Genesis), had been given this magical knowledge, which would later be called Enochian Magic. Dee believed that the path of Enochian Magic was a very high spiritual path and that it was a person's birthright. In a sense, he believed it to be a bridge between the higher spiritual worlds and the physical world (recall the saying "as above, so below"). As far as we know, Dee never attempted to contact any evil or lower angels or entities and always directed his communications to the higher angels of God.

Eventually, Dee established communications with these angels with the assistance of a scryer named Edward Kelley. Scrying is when someone looks into a crystal ball (such as the one illustrated in plate 4 of the color insert) and sees scenes by psychic or clairvoyant powers; what he sees may reveal the future or the past or give him answers to his questions or both. Scrying can also be done using cups filled with water or using black mirrors. It can even be done by looking into fire or smoke. Scrying was a common practice in ancient times, and many believe Nostradamus used this divination technique as well.

Kelley was a clairvoyant who, by gazing into his crystal ball, could see other worlds and their inhabitants—in this case, angels. The highlight of these communications was a series of Calls, or strange words in the Enochian language, which were revealed to Dee and Kelley. When recited, these Calls opened up the thirty higher Aethyrs or spiritual worlds described earlier.

Figure 1.1. Black mirrors, also used for scrying, are generally made of obsidian. Dr. Dee had an obsidian mirror.

Unfortunately, after Enochian Magic resurfaced with Dee, it was to disappear again for centuries.

Dr. Dee's research into the occult relied heavily on the work of another famous magician, Henry Cornelius Agrippa, whose belief in God was as strong as Dee's. Agrippa is considered to have written a definitive text on magic, *Three Books of Occult Philosophy;* Dee had a copy of this work near him whenever he performed an angelic communication. I own one of the few surviving copies of this book that was published in 1651 (the first English edition). Many magicians and scholars believe it to be the most important book in the history of occultism in the West, and many if not all modern magical groups, like the Golden Dawn,* have consistently drawn upon its magical treasures.

Agrippa intended that his book be a path to God and be used for the spiritual good of all. I believe Agrippa's main goal was to obtain mystical union with God, and he felt that his book would be important in helping others achieve that goal. He told a friend that he felt everyone should experience mystical union with God. He believed attitude was very important in magic, and he felt that you needed to have a proper spiritual attitude to protect yourself from evil spirits or demons. Both he and Dr. Dee believed that the ancients were aware of this spiritual magic and practiced it. Agrippa states in the beginning of his book that

> Magick is a faculty of a wonderful virtue, full of most high mysteries, containing the most profound Contemplation of most secret things, together with the nature, power, quality, substance, and vertues thereof, as also the knowledge of whole nature . . . it produceth its wonderfull effects. . . . This is the most perfect and chief Science, that sacred and sublime kind of Philosophy.[1]

## The Scientific Basis of Magic

It's my belief that the Enochian language, which opens up spiritual realms for us, works in a sense like a mantra and causes an altered state of consciousness. Magic may not be as supernatural as we think, but it functions according to a higher level of a law of the universe, which we're not yet privy to. Just as Newton was not aware of the Theory of Relativity, things that we believe to be miracles (or magic) may be

---

*The Hermetic Order of the Golden Dawn (or, more commonly, the Golden Dawn) was a magical order founded in Great Britain during the late nineteenth century; it practiced theurgy and spiritual development. It has been one of the largest single influences on twentieth-century Western occultism.

manifestations of higher laws not yet discovered. (Perhaps there is no such thing as "the supernatural" because everything is really a part of a higher law existing in a higher spiritual realm.)

## The Enochian Calls

One of the keys to Enochian Magic is the Enochian Calls you will recite. Because these Calls were so powerful, the angels sometimes gave them to Dr. Dee in the reverse order in which they were to be recited so as not to upset the process of communication.

Since the time of Dr. Dee, no one has really known how to properly pronounce the Enochian words of the Calls. Israel Regardie of the Golden Dawn and Aleister Crowley of the Ordo Templi Orientis (OTO) have developed their own interpretations. Other groups have also experimented with them and have used their own versions, most likely adapted from books about Dr. Dee and his angelic communications.

In researching this book, I studied the British Library's original scans of Dee's manuscripts. I found that, in the margins of Dee's diaries, he broke up the words of the Calls and included accents on them indicating how he thought they should be pronounced. I've incorporated these pronunciations into the Calls reprinted in this book and you can also hear them on the accompanying CD found at the back of the book. I believe that my version of these pronunciations is the most accurate since the sixteenth century and the time of Dr. Dee. They are key to opening the doors to the thirty Aethyrs or higher spiritual dimensions.

Some people have said that it's not that important to be able to pronounce them so accurately, but I disagree. You must realize that, if magic is producing an effect in the higher realms, it will reflect down into the physical realms (as above, so below). Specific sounds produce specific resonances. Like mantras in meditation, the pronunciation of the Calls needs to be precise because they cause neurological changes and resonances in our physical and spiritual bodies. I believe these changes are very positive; your physical, mental, and spiritual bodies will all benefit from them. You will also notice a much clearer mental focus after performing this magic meditation; it's as if your entire being were refreshed. This is a side benefit in addition to the main one of being able to enter the higher spheres or Aethyrs and make contact with the angels found there.

## The Proper Use of Magic

I hope you will agree with my viewpoint that magic in its original form was never intended to manipulate the spiritual world and the angels for personal benefit. Let me give you an example of how asking for something that you think is good may turn out to be against the will of God. Let's say you're out of work, and you have a large family and are in a terrible financial situation. It's so bad that you're in danger of losing your house, and you don't have enough money to get by. In your magic ritual, you ask for money, which seems like a good intention because it's for your family and it's a necessity.

Magic works by using natural laws and circumstances to bring about the desired effect. The money will not fall from heaven, but circumstances will occur to bring it to you. So, you do your magic, and a few weeks later, you find out your uncle was killed in car accident and he left you a large sum of money. Well, you got your wish, but is it possible that your uncle would still be alive if you had never asked for the money? Who knows? Maybe he would have died at that instant anyway, and the asking was part of all of this.

In this case, perhaps it would have been better not to ask for money in a magic ritual, but to ask for what you want in a prayer to God instead. (I always ask him to help me attain my desire only if it's his will to accomplish this for me.) I do believe that prayer is important, and asking for things in prayer is different from asking for them as part of a magic ritual. Magic is something else again; it's powerful and can manipulate spiritual and physical forces, so you must be careful with it.

The following is another example of the consequences of using magic. Your grandmother is very ill. In your magical ritual, you ask that she be healed and not die. Maybe it was her time to die, and that was God's will, but your magic circumvented that, and now she recovers. She is well enough to drive and has an accident with a school bus, and many children are injured. Maybe this would not have happened, and many suffered because of your magic. Again, who knows if this would have happened anyway, but I just want to make clear my philosophy on asking for things in magic. You must be very careful what you ask for as you may get it, and that may not be such a good thing in the end.

Before I end this chapter, I want to add a personal comment. I've been on a spiritual search for over forty years. I actually started in high school when I took my first Zen meditation class. I was initiated into Transcendental Meditation (TM) in 1973 and studied with Eastern masters and teachers; I was involved in almost every known organized religion and studied and practiced metaphysics and occult teachings— such as astrology, spiritualism, scrying, astral projection, séances, and meditation.

To be honest, I've had some very interesting metaphysical experiences, but nothing that compares to what I've experienced since I started practicing the Enochian Magic I will be teaching you. In this book, I can't guarantee you will have the same success that I've had, since we're all different physically, mentally, and spiritually. I do believe, however, that I will be giving you the best tools available for you to be successful.

This book provides a very powerful and effective technique. It's up to you to treat it with respect and use it well. I believe that the use of prayer is always important at the beginning and end of anything highly spiritual and powerful. That's the way Dr. Dee lived his life and practiced his magic. He never started or ended a magical session without saying many prayers and invocations. I believe your attitude and intentions are extremely important to the success of this magic. There is a saying that if you take one step toward God, he will take ten steps toward you. I believe magic is one step we can take toward God.

I wish you the best on your spiritual path toward God and hope that Enochian Magic will play a significant role in the unfolding of your spiritual life.

# 2

# MAGIC IN THE BIBLE

The Bible has been one of the bestselling books in the world for an untold number of years. No one really knows how many copies of it have actually been purchased, but the estimates are staggering: some claim the figure is over a hundred million copies. *Business Week,* in its July 2005 issue, claimed that a total of 2.5 billion copies of the Bible have been sold. Other estimates put the total of Bible sales at over six billion copies. It's been translated into almost every known language (some estimate this number of languages to be in excess of two thousand) and is the most revered and criticized book in the world.

Almost all Christians and Jews base their belief system on the Bible, and even our laws and customs are founded on its principles (i.e., the Ten Commandments and the laws in the Books of Exodus and Leviticus). The founding fathers of the United States, most of whom were Christians, based the principles of the Declaration of Independence and Bill of Rights on the Bible. It doesn't matter whether someone believes in it as the inspired word of God or not; it still has influenced just about every person in the United States today.

## Magic in the Old Testament

What most people don't realize is that magic is a consistent feature of the Bible, especially the Old Testament. It was a part of normal religious experience and daily life at that time. I will give specific examples, but first I must discuss the erroneous view that the Bible condemns the practice of all magic. The key word here is all. There are many forms of magic, including black magic and white magic, and there are all kinds in between.

For argument's sake, let's say there are ten different kinds of magic, and two of them are considered black or evil magic. The Bible does condemn these two forms, but it accepts the use and practice of the other eight. So, many think that, since some forms of magic (black or evil) are condemned in the Bible, all forms of magic are. As we shall see, this is definitely not true. In fact, and as stated earlier in this book, most forms of magic were accepted forms of religious practice for many, if not all, of the biblical patriarchs—including Abraham, Moses, and Joseph. The Bible is very clear on this, and the examples are numerous.

Another reason for the confusion is that the Bible uses two different words for spiritual entities, *daimon* and *diabolos*. *Diabolos* refers to God's adversary, which we call Satan. *Daimon* refers to all other spiritual entities and beings, many of whom are good. Unfortunately, the early English translations of the Bible, including the King James version, have translated these two different terms as one term, *diabolos*, thereby lumping the good angels, the bad angels, and spiritual entities together erroneously.

I think it would be interesting to point out what the first magical act is in the Bible and who performed it. A good friend of mine by the name of Marty Stuart made an important observation. He told me that God performed the first magical act when he created the heavens and the earth. To do this, he first conceived the idea and then spoke the words, and everything was created. This certainly sounds like magic to me. Magic uses words and ideas to cause changes in both the spiritual and physical world. I know many people don't like to think that God uses magic, but the point is that the creation of heaven and the earth is described by the writer of Genesis as being similar to a magical act. Thus, the author of Genesis must have been familiar with magic to use this analogy.

Also, what about the tree of knowledge of good and evil and the Tree of Life; they certainly sound like magical trees. One bestows knowledge when its fruit is consumed, and one gives eternal life. (I wish I'd had something like that in college before I took my exams!) Again, to me this is a very clear example of a writer trying to tell a story (of how sin entered the world and why humans are mortal) using the motif of magic and magical principles. I'm not saying these examples illustrate real historical events; I'm saying that the writer of the Bible treated them as if they were magical events.

Divination is considered an essential part of magic, and I will discuss this in more detail later. But for now, I want to look at some specific examples of divination in the Bible.* In Exodus 28:29–30, we have the following statement:

> So Aaron shall bear the names of the sons of Israel in the breastpiece of judgment on his heart, when he goes into the Holy Place, to bring them to regular remembrance before the Lord. And in the breastpiece of judgment you shall put the Urim and the Thummim, and they shall be on Aaron's heart, when he goes in before the Lord. Thus Aaron shall bear the judgment of the people of Israel on his heart before the Lord regularly.

The "Urim" and "Thummim" were devices used for magical divination or for discovering the will of God. No one knows exactly what these devices were, but there has been much speculation about them. Some think they were just two stones or gems, with the Hebrew word or symbol for "yes" on one and "no" on the other. If you wanted to find out what the will of God was, you would ask a question and draw one of the stones. They could have also simply been two stones, one white and one black. Others think they could have been twenty-two

---

*Unless otherwise indicated, the scripture quotations in this book are from The Holy Bible, English Standard Version (ESV), copyright 2001 by Crossway Bibles, a publishing ministry of Good News Publishers, used with permission. All rights reserved.

stones, each inscribed with one letter of the Hebrew alphabet. Thus it would work something like an Ouija board in that it would spell out the answer instead of just a simple yes or no. Please keep in mind that this procedure of divination using the Urim and the Thummim is mentioned in several places in the Old Testament (Exodus 28:30, Leviticus 8:8, Numbers 27:21, Deuteronomy 33:8, 1 Samuel 28:6, Ezra 2:63, and Nehemiah 7:65), and each time it's considered an accepted form of religious practice, designed to determine what God wanted the people of Israel to do.

If this isn't magic, I don't know what it is. Whether you believe it worked or not isn't the point. The point is that *they* believed it worked and they believed it worked by magic. The priests, who were God's representatives on earth, used this divination process to ascertain God's will for his people. Would the church today accept a priest using an ouija board or a pendulum (the direction it swings indicating yes or no to a question posed) to make a decision?

We see another example of Urim and Thummim being used in Numbers 27:21, where the Lord tells Moses to take Joshua and give him some of his authority so he can stand before the Lord and inquire (using Urim and Thummim):

> And he shall stand before Eleazar the priest, who shall inquire for him by the judgment of the Urim before the Lord. At his word they shall go out, and at his word they shall come in, both he and all the people of Israel with him, the whole congregation.

Notice something important here. This practice isn't something that anyone can do. Only a priest, and most likely, a high priest, is authorized to practice this magic. Other interesting references are:

> Give to Levi your Thummim, and your Urim to your godly one. . . .
> DEUTERONOMY 33:8

The governor told them that they were not to partake of the most holy food, until there should be a priest to consult Urim and Thummim.

Ezra 2:63

Other types of divination are also mentioned, but whether they employed the Urim and Thummim or some other ritual object or device isn't known. Other ritual objects may have been some pieces of wood or paper with something inscribed on them. Examples are:

The lot is cast into the lap, but its every decision is from the Lord.

Proverbs 16:33

The lot puts an end to quarrels and decides between powerful contenders.

Proverbs 18:18

The first quote has very strong positive words regarding divination: "every decision is from the Lord." The second quote shows the positive value of divination in that it prevents contention and quarrels.

One of my favorite references to divination is its use by Joseph, with whom everyone is familiar. In Genesis, chapters thirty-seven and thirty-nine, we find the story of how Joseph was sold into slavery to the Egyptians because his brothers were jealous of him; their father liked him the best and treated him better than his other sons. (This story has frequently been depicted in church plays and features the multi-colored coat that Joseph's father had given him.) As the story goes, after Joseph was sold into slavery in Egypt, he rose to power there and was the second highest in command. (Only the Pharaoh was above him.) Years later, when there was a famine in Egypt, his brothers were sent to Egypt by their father to buy grain, and unknowingly, they appeared before Joseph. He didn't reveal his identity to them but gave them grain to take back. In so doing, Joseph gave the following orders to his steward:

Fill the men's sacks with food, as much as they can carry, and put each man's money in the mouth of his sack, and put my cup, the silver cup, in the mouth of the sack of the youngest, with his money for the grain.

GENESIS 44:1–2

Joseph is playing games with his brothers when he orders his steward, after they have left, to go after them and inspect their sacks. The steward is then instructed to accuse the brothers of stealing Joseph's special cup.

They had gone only a short distance from the city. Now Joseph said to his steward, "Up, follow after the men, and when you overtake them, say to them, 'Why have you repaid evil for good? Is it not from this that my lord drinks, and by this that he practices divination? You have done evil in doing this.'"

GENESIS 44:4–5

Here we have one of the most famous patriarchs of the Bible owning and using a divination cup! This is clear indication that practices of this type were not only condoned but used frequently by priests and rulers to ascertain the will of God in their affairs and the affairs of their kingdom.

My guess is that this cup was used for scrying.

## Examples of Black Magic in the Bible

There are several examples of what I take to be the practice of black magic in the Bible. One example from the Old Testament discusses a practice that a legitimate priest would perform. To me it sounds like black magic, but I'll let you be the judge. It occurs in Numbers 5:11–31 and pertains to wives who are unfaithful. Basically, if a man believed that his wife had been unfaithful but there were no witnesses or proof, the following ritual would be performed. Gathering dust from the floor of the tabernacle, the priest would make a concoction of it and water and who knows what else. (Dust was included because, being from the Tabernacle, it represented the presence of God.)

> And the priest shall set the woman before the Lord and unbind the hair of the woman's head and place in her hands the grain offering of remembrance, which is the grain offering of jealousy. And in his hand the priest shall have the water of bitterness that brings the curse.
>
> NUMBERS 5:18

The accused women would drink this concoction, while the priest recited some words over her.

> Then the priest shall make her take an oath, saying, "If no man has lain with you, and if you have not turned aside to uncleanness while you were under your husband's authority, be free from this water of bitterness that brings the curse. But if you have gone astray, though you're under your husband's authority, and if you have defiled yourself, and some man other than your husband has lain with you, then" (let the priest make the woman take the oath of the curse, and say to the woman) "the Lord make you a curse and an oath among your people, when the Lord makes your thigh fall away and your body swell. May this water that brings the curse pass into your bowels and make your womb swell and your thigh fall away." And the woman shall say, "Amen, Amen."
>
> NUMBERS 5:19–22

I like the explicitness of the King James version better, which ends by saying "make your belly to swell and your thigh to rot."

Here we have curses and potions that sound like black magic to me, and yet this was an accepted practice of the Israelites and performed by the priest to ascertain if a woman had committed adultery. (It's interesting that there is no test for a man's infidelity.)

Another story that contains what sounds like black magic appears in 2 Kings 2:23–24. The great prophet Elisha, who was bald, was on a road to the town of Bethel. Some youths from the city came out and mocked him:

> He went up from there to Bethel, and while he was going up on the way, some small boys came out of the city and jeered at him, saying, "Go up, you baldhead! Go up, you baldhead!"
>
> 2 KINGS 2:23

Now the great prophet Elisha utters a curse on these young boys:

> And he turned around, and when he saw them, he cursed them in the name of the Lord. And two she-bears came out of the woods and tore forty-two of the boys.
>
> 2 KINGS 2:24

The King James version says "tare forty and two children of them."

This sounds more like black magic than white magic to me. When is the last time you uttered a curse to kill someone because they teased you? I realize we cannot put our twenty-first-century values on an ancient culture, but this is clearly an indication that magic was used by well-respected and revered patriarchs of the Bible. And these are not single occurrences but everyday affairs. There isn't anything in the Bible to indicate that these practices were considered wrong or evil. The priests were like gods, and if they performed these rituals, the rituals must have been acceptable because they were considered to be from God. So, before we use the Bible as proof that all magic is wrong, reflect on the examples and passages cited above.

## Other Examples of Magic in the Bible

There are numerous other examples of magic in the Bible, and we will look at a few of the more well-known ones.

Moses was one of the most famous magicians of the Bible and performed many miracles, or should I say magic. He caused plagues of frogs, lice, and flies; changed his staff into a serpent; made livestock become diseased; turned river water into blood; brought down hail, locusts, and darkness; created a plague of boils on people and beasts alike; and finally, uttered a curse that would kill all of the firstborn in the land of Egypt. God certainly kept Moses busy with all of these miracles (or should I say magical rituals). Moses did have to perform a ritual to produce all of these effects, such as holding up his staff and uttering certain words. Some people claim that these were miracles and not magic; they define a miracle as an event produced or caused by the direct intervention of God. Magic, on the other hand, is produced by a person's ability to manipulate the spiritual realm and the angels. Can we really determine what is caused by God, what is a natural occurrence, and what is the direct result of magic?

Now we will look at a biblical story in which there is no question that ritual magic was involved. Catholics have seven books in their Old Testament that the Protestants don't include in their canon. One of these books is the Book of Tobit. This story begins with the description of an Israelite living in the city of Nineveh in the eighth century BCE. He had been blinded by bird droppings that fell in his eyes. He decided to send his son Tobias to Media to collect some money that was rightfully his.

In this story, there is also a woman named Sarah who lives in Media. She was married seven times, and each time, her husband was killed on their wedding night by the demon Asmodeus. Asmodeus was considered to be the demon of lust. The story doesn't explain why all Sarah's husbands on their wedding night were killed by this demon. (Nice girl to take home to mother!) The angel Raphael is sent by God to help both Tobit and Sarah. Raphael disguises himself as a man and offers to be a guide and protector for Tobias during his trip to Media, and Tobias agrees to this, unaware that Raphael is really an angel. While traveling to Media with Raphael, Tobias is attacked by a giant fish, which he captures and drags to the land. He is instructed by Raphael to remove the heart, liver, and gallbladder of this fish. He asks Raphael why he should do this and Raphael says:

> And he said unto him, touching the heart and the liver, if a devil or an evil spirit trouble any, we must make a smoke thereof before the man or the woman, and the party shall be no more vexed. As for the gall, it is good to anoint a man that hath whiteness in his eyes, and he shall be healed.
>
> TOBIT 6: 7–8 (AUTHORIZED KING JAMES VERSION)

When they reach Media, Raphael brings Tobias and Sarah together to be married and tells him to burn the fish liver and heart on their wedding night. This will prevent the demon from killing Tobias.

> And when thou shalt come into the marriage chamber, thou shalt take the ashes of perfume, and shalt lay upon them some of the heart and liver of the fish, and shalt make a smoke with it. And the devil shall smell it, and flee away, and never come again any more.
>
> TOBIT 6:16–17 (AV)

The demon Asmodeus is driven away, and all is well with Tobias and Sarah on their wedding night. Upon arriving home to Ninevah with his new wife, Raphael instructs Tobias to use the gallbladder to heal his father's blindness, which he does, and his father is cured.

> And took hold of his father: and he strake of the gall on his father's eyes, saying, Be of good hope, my father. And when his eyes began

to smart, he rubbed them; And the whiteness pilled away from the corners of his eyes: and when he saw his son, he fell upon his neck.

TOBIT 11:11–13 (AV)

Thus, there is a happy ending to this story because of the use of ritual magic.

Another example of biblical magic is from the Book of Ezekiel. Nebuchadnezzar, the king of Babylon, is with his army at a highway that divides into two roads. One leads to Judah and the other to Ammon. Both the people of Judah and the people of Ammon have plotted against him, and he wants to destroy them both. He needs to know which country the gods want him to destroy first so he can be successful. To accomplish this, he uses divination:

For the king of Babylon stands at the parting of the way, at the head of the two ways, to use divination. He shakes the arrows; he consults the teraphim; he looks at the liver.

EZEKIEL 21:21

He decides to use three different types of divination and see what each foretells. The first type, called "shaking the arrows" (known as belomancy), was, as its name implies, a process that utilized arrows. In one form of belomancy, two marked arrows—one with the name Judah on it and the other enscribed with the name Ammon—were placed in a quiver. One arrow was randomly drawn, and this one indicated which country should be attacked first. A second method of belomancy involved more arrows which, when thrown from a quiver, would form a pattern that could be read. This was akin to reading tea leaves, but in this case, arrows were utilized instead of tea leaves.

The second type of divination that Nebuchadnezzar employed used idols or teraphim. These manufactured idols or "household gods" (as teraphim is translated) were commonly utilized in Old Testament times for divination, both in the Mesopotamia region and in Palestine. (See Genesis

Figure 2.1. A clay model of a sheep's liver used in divination in Babylon, 2000 BCE

31:19 and Judges 17:5.) No one really knows how this operated, but my speculation is that these household gods were made of crystal or glass, and scrying (crystal gazing) was the method employed. Unfortunately, the specifics of this type of divination have not come down to us.

The third type of divination used by Nebuchadnezzar involved an animal's organ, specifically a liver and most likely a sheep's liver. A sheep was sacrificed and cut open, and the color and shape of its liver was analyzed. If there were any peculiar marks, these were analyzed as well. This type of divination was very common in Babylon (as well as in Rome); inscriptions found on Babylonian monuments frequently allude to it.

For more examples of magic contained in the Bible, we can look to the Book of Daniel. Some biblical scholars classify Daniel as a magician and an astrologer. He also had the ability to interpret dreams. He interpreted several dreams of King Nebuchadnezzar. Daniel 5:11 states the following:

There is a man in your kingdom in whom is the spirit of the holy gods. In the days of your father, light and understanding and wisdom like the wisdom of the gods were found in him, and King Nebuchadnezzar, your father—your father the king—made him chief of the magicians, enchanters, Chaldeans, and astrologers.

DANIEL 5:11

A very interesting and often debated incident occurred when the Israelites were wandering in the wilderness after they had left Egypt. At one point, many serpents appeared in their path, and numerous people were bitten and died. When this happened, God told Moses to make an image of a serpent and put it on a pole. He further instructed that whoever was bitten should look at this image and they would be cured:

So Moses made a bronze serpent and set it on a pole. And if a serpent bit anyone, he would look at the bronze serpent and live.

NUMBERS 21:9

This was a magical remedy that God gave to Moses. The image, which represented the snake, would either cause the removal of the venom or it would inactivate it. In a sense, this bronze serpent was a magic amulet for snakebites. This type of magic is called "sympathetic magic," in which the principle "likes produce likes" is operating. This has also been called "the law of similarity."

Another interesting story involving sympathetic magic occurs in Genesis in the story of Jacob and how he served his father-in-law, Laban, in the country of Padan Aram. Jacob made a deal with Laban, which was that he would care for Laban's flock in exchange for receiving its speckled and spotted sheep and goats (of which there were only a few) for himself. Based on his knowledge of sympathetic magic, Jacob did the following: He took green rods or branches, peeled strips off of them, and exposed the white from the rods. He then put the branches in front of a watering trough where the flock came to drink. This caused them to conceive offspring that were streaked, speckled, and spotted.

The boat builder Noah is probably a good candidate for classification as a magician as well. How do you think he got all those animals into the ark? Legend says when Adam and Eve sinned and were naked, God had to sacrifice an animal or animals so that they would have skins to cover themselves with:

> And the Lord God made for Adam and for his wife garments of skins and clothed them.
>
> GENESIS 3:21

Because the hand of God had made these animal skins for Adam and Eve, these skins had magical properties. They were passed down from Adam to his son Seth and to the other patriarchs until they wound up in the possession of Noah. Legend has it that, when Noah wore the skins, it gave him power over the animals, and thus, he was able to command them to go into the ark.

In the Bible there are also examples of magic that was condemned.

> There shall not be found among you anyone who burns his son or his daughter as an offering, anyone who practices divination or tells fortunes or interprets omens, or a sorcerer or a charmer or a medium or a necromancer or one who inquires of the dead, for whoever does these things is an abomination to the Lord. And because of these abominations the Lord your God is driving them out before you.
>
> DEUTERONOMY 18:10–12

Different authors wrote various parts of the Bible, so the passage above may have been written by an author or editor who, for some reason, didn't care for anything of an occult nature. On the other hand, if we look closely at the terms used above, it appears that most of the occult practices mentioned fall into the category of black magic (a son or daughter must pass through fire; witchcraft, sorcery, or the casting of spells transpires; or the dead are contacted). Thus, I believe this is an indictment of black or evil magic but not of *all* magic and divination practices.

Another example of magic that's condemned in the Bible is found in 1 Samuel 28:3–15 in which King Saul consults with a medium, the Witch of Endor, and asks her to bring up the spirit of Samuel. This is definitely a taboo practice, and in fact, the spirit of Samuel rebuked Saul for doing this. The calling up of deceased spirits is necromancy and is clearly prohibited in the Bible.

These examples illustrate the point that I made at the beginning of this chapter. There was magic that was acceptable and frequently practiced in the religious lives of the Israelites. Much of this magic was necessary ritual for the priests. There were also certain forms of magic that were not allowed and were condemned such as witchcraft, necromancy, and human sacrifice.

Now I can ask the question: "Why was it so important for these ancient peoples to use magic and divination?" The Israelites, especially, wanted to know the will of God. Remember, they were the chosen people, and they believed that they existed to do the will of God, which would help them survive and prosper. For example, if they were going into battle against a certain nation, it would be advantageous for them to know if they were going to win or lose the battle. If the divination said they would lose, most likely they would not fight but sue for peace. Magic, divination, and prophecy were left in the hands of the specialist, the priest, who was thought of as being closest to God. Also, they were the only individuals who could enter the Holy of Holies in the Tabernacle.

In the next chapter, we will be looking at the magical practices of other ancient civilizations, and we will come to see that there are many similarities between them and the magic practiced by the Israelites. In fact, the Israelites probably learned most of their magical practices from neighboring civilizations, such as the Akkadians, Assyrians, Babylonians, and the Egyptians. Other cultures of that time also believed that God or the gods controlled everything, and they believed that knowing the will of God or the gods could help them to survive and prosper.

We have seen that certain types of divination were accepted, and other types were prohibited. We have also learned that some practices that were accepted in the Bible seemed almost if not entirely to be forms of black magic. Some scholars have attempted to draw a dividing line between these methods, but I think it varied over time. One practice may have been acceptable in one time and not in another—or, one in one place (like the Northern Kingdom of Israel), and not in another (the Southern Kingdom of Judah).

It's interesting that the Dead Sea Scrolls contain examples of magic used by the Qumran community. These examples described divination and astrology, and it's clear that this community practiced and believed in these forms of magic. Angelic invocations are also found in the Dead Sea Scrolls.

In conclusion, it was not only the Hebrews mentioned in the Bible that practiced magic in order to ascertain the will of God but other cultures and religious groups as well.

# 3

# MAGIC IN ANCIENT
# CIVILIZATIONS

We will now explore other ancient civilizations, which employed magic. These include the Sumerians, the Akkadians, the Assyrians, the Babylonians, and the Egyptians. These civilizations were founded before the time of ancient Israel. The reason for discussing the ancient Israelites first, however, is because I believe that most people who are reading this book are probably more familiar with the Bible than the religious books of these other more obscure civilizations. Even though there is a difference in the beliefs and practices of magic between these more obscure civilizations and those of the Israelites, they are still, in essence, very similar.

The earliest known civilization, the Sumerians, began around seven thousand BCE in the Tigris-Euphrates Valley, known as Mesopotamia. Then came the Akkadians, and finally the Assyrians and the Babylonians. (That is an approximate chronological order with some overlapping.) Numerous Akkadian texts, many of them about magic, became known when the Royal Library of Ashurbanipal at Nineveh was unearthed in the middle of the nineteenth century. This library dates back to the seventh century BCE; its twenty-eight thousand clay tablets inscribed in cuneiform are now housed in the British Museum.

Some of these texts were the Akkadians' incantations to their gods and were also used to conjure up spirits. They included instructions as to specific words to recite, songs to sing, ritual movements of the body to make, and the proper use of incense. The goal of those invoking the magic was to attract the spirits or gods to help them or protect them from something specific, or even to control the weather or to influence other people or both.

Discovered in this library was also the Mesopotamian story of creation, called The *Enuma Elish*. It predates the Old Testament story of creation in Genesis. It was written in Akkadian on seven clay tablets using cuneiform script. This script was one of the earliest known forms of writing, which were created by the Sumerians around three thousand BCE. A blunt reed, known as a stylus, was used to make this script on the tablets.

The *Enuma Elish* is very significant because it revealed to scholars a clear understanding of how the Babylonians viewed creation. It tells

Figure 3.1. A large cuneiform tablet with inscriptions

the story of how human beings existed to serve the gods. Its chief god Marduk was supreme among all other Mesopotamian gods. The title *Enuma Elish* translates to "When on High." There has been much debate and discussion about whether the Hebrew Bible story of creation was based on the Mesopotamian story, which predated it, or a common source that was used by both. This is a controversial issue and has still not been resolved. There are many similarities between the two stories as well as many important differences. In both stories, the creation is based on the Word of God or the act of divine speech by a god. It also has major differences. In the Genesis story, there is one God—not many as found in the Babylonian story—and this one God doesn't act frivolously like the gods in the *Enuma Elish* story do.

The civilizations of Mesopotamia also practiced magic, and in fact, there are many examples of magic used by the Mesopotamians in the Bible. I believe that much of the magical practices of the Hebrews were taken from these Mesopotamian civilizations and adapted and modified for their own use.

## Important Cultural Distinctions

How was the magic of the Israelites different from that of these other civilizations in this region? We know that the Israelites based their society and government on a theocracy (*theo* meaning God), whereby God was the head or ruler of the people. By using divination, oracles, and other practices, the priests could ask God questions and supposedly get solid answers.

The surrounding peoples (the Sumerians, Akkadians, Babylonians, Assyrians, and Egyptians) also had similar beliefs, but the difference was that they were polytheistic, meaning that they believed in many gods that ruled nature and the universe. There were gods of the stars, sun, moon, wind, mountains, streams, rivers, and oceans. You name it, it had its own god. Their magic was more diverse and varied in that they used it not only to ascertain what a certain god may have wanted them to do but to manipulate that god to do what they wanted *it* to do.

For example, if there was a drought, they would perform some ritual or magic for the rain god, trying to get it to cause it to rain. They had to know something about the gods so they studied nature to ascertain what the gods were like—their characteristics, how to attract them, and most importantly, how to control them. They also observed the cyclical nature of the seasons and life in general, and as a result, their magic was more cyclical in character than that of the Israelites. We will see these differences when we explore their magic.

There were special priests in these other civilizations that performed magic, as did the Hebrew priests, but it appears that the common people were also involved in magic and didn't always have to rely on the priests in order to practice it.

Another difference, as stated above, was that the god of the Israelites was not a frivolous god—but a just, good, infinite, and loving god. He was perfect, in fact infinitely perfect, and he was most holy. The gods of these other civilizations appeared to have qualities that were more akin to those of humans: they were jealous, frivolous, and petty. These gods fought among themselves and did things that we humans would never consider doing. The magic of these civilizations was very much involved with trying to appease these gods and circumvent them from causing harm or problems. Thus, these cultures had a different approach to magic than the Hebrews did.

The flood narratives of the two societies show their different views of God or the gods. In both the Old Testament and the religious books of the Sumerians (the Epic of Gilgamesh) there is a universal flood. Like the creation stories, we don't know whether the Israelites and the Sumerians both drew their stories from a common source. We find similarities in both flood stories in that only a few people are saved in a boat that the hero is asked to build. In addition, there is a sacrifice to God or the gods at the end.

In the Israelite story, God destroys the earth because of its wickedness. He is a just God, and it grieves his heart to realize that there is so much evil and violence in the world. In order to cleanse the earth and its peoples, he brings about the flood and saves only the just and righteous Noah and his family. In the Epic of Gilgamesh, humans are making too much noise and are bothering the peace of the gods, which angers them. The gods then decide to destroy humankind with a flood. There is a huge difference in the character of each of their gods.

Certain magical practices or rituals could be good magic in one society and evil in another. Let's examine the Genesis story of Adam and Eve in the garden with the snake. There is a similar story in the Babylonian culture having to do with the Garden of Eden. Tablets found at El-Amarna tell a story similar to the Genesis story but with a twist. The first human in this story is named Adapa (the Babylonian Adam). He is mortal, although he is the son of the god Ea. He is summoned to appear before the God of Heaven. His father Ea decides to give Adapa advice before he appears before the God of Heaven. He warns Adapa that he will be offered the Bread and Water of Death and that he should not eat or drink it.

When Adapa appears before the God of Heaven, he is offered the bread and water his father warned him of, and he doesn't consume it. Unfortunately, however, it's not the Bread and Water of Death that he has been offered but of eternal life. Thus, he misses the opportunity to become immortal. Eating the fruit in the Garden of Eden prevented Adam from gaining eternal life and immortality, and *not* eating the bread and water in the Babylonian story prevented Adapa from gaining eternal life. Maybe these two similar stories came from a common source, but each had its own interpretion and ending.

# The Importance of Magic

Why is it important to have a general understanding of the history and practice of magic in ancient civilizations? Everyone knows the people were mostly pagans, and it's no shock that they believed and practiced ritual magic. The point is that throughout most of human history, the belief and practice of magic was widespread. It's only recently, within a narrow time frame of a few hundred years, that many people have decided that magic is nonsense. It follows that they believe that the people of these ancient civilizations were superstitious and primitive.

This bias, however, isn't accepted by all anthropologists and researchers. Many believe these ancient civilizations, especially the Egyptians, had knowledge and wisdom that's unmatched today. Just look at the Great Pyramid of Giza. We couldn't build a pyramid like that, with its degree of precision, using our modern equipment and technology. We can also look at other monuments, such as Stonehenge, the Nasca Lines, and those found at other ancient sites. Are these the products of a primitive society, or did that society's members have access to secret knowledge that we don't have?

Even if they didn't possess advanced science and technology, maybe they had reached a higher spiritual level than we have. Maybe they were able to master forces, such as psychic powers and levitation. Before we judge them, we should examine many unanswered questions having to do with their use of magic, which may ultimately be a clue in answering these imponderables.

# The Very First Forms of Magic

I discussed the magical beliefs and practices of the ancient Israelites. Now I will step back in time to the beginning of the human race and uncover the first forms of magic. H. P. Blavatsky, the well-known theosophist of the nineteenth century, said that magic is as old as humankind itself and it's impossible to name a time or epoch when it didn't exist.

Some anthropologists believe that magic may have originated when primitive humans felt threatened by either real or imaginary ghosts or evil beings. To protect themselves from these supernatural beings, they developed rituals and what we call magical practices in response to these threats. These rituals may have taken the form of hand gestures, vocal sounds or yelling, dancing, the throwing of objects, or several of these actions. To these people, there were good spirits and bad spirits, and it was possible they used these rituals (magic) to control the spirits.

As civilizations developed, this belief didn't go away but, in fact, became more systematic and organized.

## Nineveh's Magical Texts

Let's look at specific examples of some of the magical texts found in the ancient library of Ashurbanipal at Nineveh. Akkadian texts contain a fair number of magical incantations. Most are divinations based on nature and natural phenomena. However, the ancient Akkadians also used animals' entrails to read the signs, such as the example cited above, in which a sheep's liver was examined by Nebuchadnezzar. Another divination method was to drop oil on water and determine what to do by reading the ensuing formation. Oil that broke or separated when hitting the water was considered a bad omen; it might mean that someone would die or fall seriously ill or that their army would be defeated and suffer heavy losses. The casting of lots was also quite popular. An interesting example of this was found in the archaeological discovery of a cube (about one inch in diameter) from the ninth century BCE, with an Akkadian inscription on it showing the selection of the minister of the Assyrian king by the drawing of lots.

Dream interpretation was also employed for divination. For instance, if someone dreamed of a black cat, it would be a good omen for that person. Divination by contacting the dead was also practiced; this was called necromancy. There is a good example of this from Mesopotamia in the story, "Enkidu and the Netherworld," from the Gilgamesh Epic, in which the ghost of Enkidu is commanded to rise from the ground. This practice was not permitted in Israel, as we saw in the example cited earlier of Saul and Samuel.

In Akkadian literature, we also have examples of sick and dying individuals using magic to try to achieve healing through prayers that are similar to the psalms of the Bible but incorporate magic rituals and words.

Other examples of divination used in the Akkadian literature include observing the heavens, stars, planets, and eclipses—as well as weather conditions and the movement and formation of the clouds, the directions of the wind, and the directions birds flew. In fact, the observation of the stars and planets led to the development of astrology, which had its beginnings in Mesopotamia. The earliest known astrological data are from approximately 2300 BCE.

The Akkadians were also the first to associate the names of gods with certain planets and stars. This is still done today with modern magic. The following is an example of a magical incantation addressed to a star named Sibziana (possibly the star Regulus). The purpose of this incantation was to induce Sibziana (a male deity of that star) to remove the evil spells, bewitchment, and possessions that typically occurred after the lunar eclipse.

O Sibziana . . .*
Thou that changest the . . .
In the heavens . . .
They bow down before thee . . .
The great gods beseech thee and . . .
Without thee Anu . . .

---

*The ". . ." indicate missing sections of the text.

Il the arbiter . . .

Ramman the prince of heaven and earth . . .

At thy command mankind was named!

Give thou the word and with thee let the great gods stand!

Give thou my judgment, make my decision!

I, thy servant, Assurbanipal, the son of his god,

Whose god is Assur, whose goddess is Assuritu,

In the evil of the eclipse of the moon which in the month [space] on
    the day [space] has taken place,

In the evil of the powers, of the portents, evil and not good,

Which are in my palace and my land,

Because of the evil magic, the disease that's not good, the iniquity,

The transgression, the sin that's in my body . . .

[Because of] the evil spectre that's bound to me and . . .

Have petitioned thee, I've glorified thee!

The raising of my hand accept! Hearken to my prayer!

Free me from my bewitchment! Loosen my sin![1]

## Egyptian Magic

Now that I've discussed magic in the area of Mesopotamia, let's move on
to the Egyptians, the next culture to develop magic. It would seem to be
obvious that, since the ancient Egyptians succeeded the Mesopotamian
cultures, the Egyptians borrowed heavily from Mesopotamean magical practices and beliefs. I would like to quote from *Egyptian Magic*
by E. A. Wallis Budge:

> The "magic" of the Egyptians was of two kinds: (1) that which was
> employed for legitimate purposes and with the idea of benefiting either
> the living or the dead, and (2) that which was made use of in the fur-
> therance of nefarious plots and schemes and was intended to bring
> calamities upon those against whom it was directed. In the religious
> texts and works we see how magic is made to be the handmaiden of

religion, and how it appears in certain passages side by side with the most exalted spiritual conceptions; . . . the Egyptians aimed at being able to command their gods to work for them, and to compel them to appear at their desire. These great results were to be obtained by the use of certain words which, to be efficacious, must be uttered in a proper tone of voice by a duly qualified man; such words might be written upon some substance, papyrus, precious stones, and the like, and worn on the person, when their effect could be transmitted to any distance. As almost every man, woman, and child in Egypt who could afford it wore some such charm or talisman, it's not to be wondered at that the Egyptians were at a very early period regarded as a nation of magicians and sorcerers.[2]

One misconception about the ancient Egyptians is that they were a primitive and superstitious culture and our wisdom and spiritual understanding is far more advanced and superior than theirs. I personally don't believe this is true. I believe that the ancient Egyptians' spiritual view and understanding of the universe and of life, as well as their technical skills, may have surpassed ours. There has always been a mystery and reverence associated with ancient Egypt, going as far back as ancient Greece, whose scholars traveled to Egypt to study the esoteric knowledge to be found there.

It was and is still a common belief that one may find answers to spiritual questions by studying ancient Egypt. In fact, many modern societies studying or practicing magic borrow heavily from the religious practices of the ancient Egyptians and their beliefs. From the many references in the Bible, the pyramid texts, the Book of the Dead, and other inscribed papyri and writings, we know that the Egyptians practiced many types of magic.

In fact, we know quite a bit about Egyptian magical practice because of the abundance of magical texts that have survived. One example I'm sure everyone is familiar with is the Exodus story in the Bible when Moses and Aaron first appear in front of Pharaoh to demand that Pharaoh let Moses's people go. Aaron is instructed to throw his staff or rod on the ground, and it turns into a serpent. Pharaoh then calls his sorcerers and magicians to repeat Moses's magic. They do so by throwing their rods on the ground, and these rods also becomes snakes. Thus, Pharoah's sorcerers and magicians were able to imitate Aaron's magic:

> Then Pharaoh summoned the wise men and the sorcerers, and they, the magicians of Egypt, also did the same by their secret arts. For each man cast down his staff, and they became serpents. But Aaron's staff swallowed up their staffs. Still Pharaoh's heart was hardened, and he would not listen to them, as the Lord had said.
>
> EXODUS 7:11–13

We have something very interesting in the last sentence of the quote above. The magicians of Pharaoh were able to duplicate the magic of Aaron, but Aaron's rod was more powerful in that it swallowed up their snakes. Here we have the principle that some magic is more powerful than others or some magicians are more powerful than others. This principle is illustrated very clearly in this biblical story and is a basic principle of magic.

Figure 3.2. An ancient Egyptian ankh

Figure 3.3 (above left). Front view of an ancient Egyptian scarab. This is a very interesting amulet since it shows the blending of Egyptian and Christian magic. The fish is a Christian symbol, but it is decorated with typical Egyptian symbolism. This was most likely worn around the neck for protection.

Figure 3.4 (above right). Rear view of the scarab shown in figure 3.3

We also see later in Exodus that the magicians of Egypt can imitate most of Moses's other miracles, like turning water into blood and inducing frogs to come out of the Nile, for instance. However, when Moses created the plague of gnats, they couldn't repeat this miracle. It was becoming apparent that Moses was a more powerful magician or had better magic than Pharaoh's magicians and sorcerers.

It's important to emphasize that the magicians of Egypt were priests, and as such, they were a special class of people. They were highly educated and the best that Egypt had to offer. It's my belief that individuals were selected to become priests because of their psychic ability. This was a special occupation, and the proper talent, training, and practice was needed to become a successful priest or magician. The reason priests were so important and highly revered in ancient Egypt is that the Egyptians believed that the survival of the country depended on them. Remember, if there was war, they had to know by divination which party would be victorious and what the outcome would be. They needed to know when and how to attack and any other pointers to wage or assure a successful campaign. The priests could also bring curses upon their enemies and prevent catastrophic events. They made use of rituals, spells, incantations, and amulets in the practice of their magic.

In particular, the Egyptians needed to know about the weather. They needed to know the timing of the flooding of the Nile; their crops were dependent on this. They wanted to control the weather to their benefit.

In addition to the practices I have discussed, astrology played a large role in divination and magic in ancient Egypt. The priests looked to the heavens to interpret the signs to help them decide which direction to take. The gods dwelled in the heavens, and the seven known planets each had their god, as did the stars and constellations. These astrological signs were used to predict the future. Numerology also played a large part in their magic. The numbers four, seven, and twelve had special significance to them.

Most of us are familiar with the monuments of Egypt, including the pyramids at Giza and the Sphinx. I believe that magical initiations and rituals took place in the Great Pyramid of Giza. We also know that the Egyptians believed that there was magic in their statues, and at certain times, the priests could cause the statues to speak. Numerous examples exist of magical spells and curses on papyri and on the walls of tombs and burial chambers. Some of these spells, like the ones from the Book of the Dead, could help the deceased on their travels through the netherworld. Other inscriptions were curses upon anyone entering or defacing the burial chamber.

## Ancient Egyptian Texts

The Egyptian pyramid texts are the oldest known religious or sacred writings in the world. These texts were found carved on the inner walls and chambers of several pyramids at Saqqara in Egypt. They were also carved on the stone coffins or sarcophagi inside these pyramids. Egyptologists believe they were written during the Old Kingdom, approximately 2650 to 2175 BCE. Even though they were written in the pyramids during this period, many archaeologists believe they were composed at the much earlier date of approximately 3000 BCE. (These texts should not be confused with the Book of the Dead, which evolved later from the pyramid texts; I will discuss the Book of the Dead shortly.)

Spells and directions for guiding the deceased pharaoh through his journey in the afterlife are discussed in these ancient texts. They also discuss how he could travel, especially how he could travel by flying in his spirit body. In addition, they contain spells for him to use to call the gods to help him. The specific texts from the Pyramid of Unas contain over two hundred spells, which are considered the oldest of all the written pyramid texts; they were written during the fifth dynasty. Later texts from the sixth dynasty were found in the pyramids of King Pepi I and King Pepi II. Gaston Maspero, a French Egyptologist, discovered the pyramid texts in 1881, and Samuel Mercer published the first complete translations of them in 1952. Approximately 760 spells have been recorded and published in all.

The Book of the Dead might be more accurately entitled "The Book of the Coming Forth by Day." The Book of the Dead was actually a title coined by Karl Richard Lepsius, a German Egyptologist who, in 1842, published some of these texts and gave them this name. It's thought that they were composed between 1600 and 1200 BCE. Like the pyramid texts, the Book of the Dead is a later collection of spells and procedures written to help the dead in the afterlife. (It was customary to place copies of spells and procedures, written on leather or papyrus, with the dead.) They were also inscribed on pyramids, tombs, and sarcophagi.

It appears that the pyramid texts were the source of and the primary material for composing the Book of the Dead. Unlike the pyramid texts, the Book of the Dead was not just for the exclusive use of the pharaoh but for the common person and woman also. Almost one-third of its chapters are derived from the pyramid texts. With the availability of the Book of the Dead, the average Egyptian could now have these texts painted or inscribed on his or her tomb or coffin and have his or her own manual for the afterlife.

One famous Egyptian theme in the Book of the Dead, which many people may be familiar with, is the "weighing of the heart." In this story, the deceased person's heart is weighed against a feather to judge that person's character. If his heart weighs the same as the feather, he is found righteous, and having passed the test, he joins the company of the gods. If, on the other hand, the heart weighs more than the feather, he fails; he is devoured by a monster, and his existence ends.

Words and names were powerful to the Egyptians and could produce magical and supernatural effects. The Egyptians wanted to know the true names of the gods, since to know their names was to have power or control over them. An enormous amount of magical texts from ancient Egypt has survived to help us understand the Egyptians' prevailing beliefs, practices, and rituals concerning magic. Here's an example of a spell from an Egyptian papyrus in the British Museum:

> To obtain a vision from the god Bes: Make a drawing of Bes, as shewn below, on your left hand, and envelope your hand in a strip of black cloth that has been consecrated to Isis and lie down to sleep without speaking a word, even in answer to a question. Wind the remainder of the cloth round your neck. The ink with which you write must be composed of the blood of a cow, the blood of a white dove, fresh frankincense, myrrh, black writing ink, cinnabar, mulberry juice, rain-water, and the juice of worm-wood and vetch. With this write your petition before the setting sun, saying, "Send the truthful seer out of the holy shrine, I beseech thee, Lampsuer, Sumarta, Baribas, Dardalam, Iorlex: O Lord send the sacred deity Anuth, Anuth, Salbana, Chambre, Breith, now, now, quickly, quickly, Come in this very night."[3]

Notice the strange names in this spell. The Egyptians may have been the first to use strange, magical-sounding names for the deities in their rituals.

## Greek and Roman Magic

As we move forward in time from the ancient Egyptians to the Hellenistic period of the Greeks and then on to the Romans, we find that magic continued to survive and flourish. In fact, magic was very much a part of everyday life in Greece and Rome. Rituals were both public and private; magic rites and festivals dedicated to the gods were carried out in cultic temples. Even the Jewish synagogues and Christian churches practiced some form of magic rituals. Magic still served as a connection between people and their gods.

Just as the Egyptians borrowed heavily from the Mesopotamian cultures, the Greeks during the Hellenistic period (the last three centuries BCE) borrowed heavily from both the ancient Egyptians and Mesopotamians. Many magical papyri of the Greeks survived, and their writings show their great interest in magic. Their magical formulas were recipes in which animal parts (eyes, legs, tails, etc.) were mixed with herbs and other ingredients to make a potion. Not only was it necessary to have the exact ingredients, it was essential to know the correct measurement of each one. This was very much like a science. These potions were part of rituals that also included certain body and hand gestures, movements, words, and sounds.

Roman magic was a composite of mainly Greek and Egyptian magic. The Romans essentially appropriated the Greek and Egyptian gods, assimilated them into their magic, and replicated them in their temple statues. Because of this, the magical rituals, spells, amulets, potions, and incantations of the two cultures were very similar. As was the case in ancient Egypt, it was important to know the names of the gods and the proper use of magical words to employ during a ritual or when casting a spell. In the Greco-Roman period, we also begin to see magicians invoking different kinds of spirits, both good and evil, to do their bidding.

Curses were also popular during the Greco-Roman period and numerous so-called curse tablets (*tabellae defixionum*) or binding spells have been found. One method of placing a curse on someone was to write the person's name on a piece of thin lead and inscribe it with magical words and symbols. It would then be rolled up, pierced with a nail, and buried in the ground, often near a gravesite or a battlefield where many people had been slain. The idea was to empower the spirits of the dead to harm the person that had been cursed. To add power to a curse, a piece of hair, nail, or skin from the person would be rolled up with the lead plate.

Love spells were cast in more or less the same fashion. The lead with the inscription on it would be hidden in the home of the person who was being pursued romantically. It was helpful to bind some of that person's hair with the lead also. (The discovery of dolls from the Hellenistic period, and after from Rome, has led to the conclusion that these cultures also practiced voodoo.)

Ascertaining the future by the use of oracles was extremely popular and an important part of Greek magic. The oracle was usually a woman, a priestess, through which a god or a deity would speak. I suspect this is similar to what a trance medium does today except that the entity possessing the person would be a god and not an ordinary spirit.

The most famous Greek oracle was the Oracle of Apollo at Delphi, who sat on a three-legged chair over a rocky crevasse, from which vapors emanated. (Perhaps there was a natural hot spring below or something that would produce the vapors. Or perhaps the vapors were produced from some kind of narcotic or drug. Narcotics and drugs were sometimes used in the magic of the period to aid in producing a trance.) In the trance state, the oracle would be able to see into the future and answer questions posed to her.

The Romans were heavily influenced by the magic of the Greeks. Over time, as the population grew, the need for priests increased. Many temples and sacred places sprang up, and pagan festivals and rituals abounded. This was a time when people believed that the gods controlled everything. Appeasing them and asking them for aid and guidance was, in a sense, a national pastime.

Many Roman emperors believed in the magical properties of amulets, gems, and rocks and had their own personal astrologers and magicians who practiced divination. It's interesting that, after the practice of magicians and astrologers was outlawed, some emperors, as well as some private citizens, continued to consult them in the privacy of their own homes. Also on the rise was a type of magic called theurgy, which was the summoning or invoking of good angels. (This is exactly the type of magic that I will be focusing on later on in this book.)

As in cultures before and since, curses, or the practice of black magic, were prevalent, and as a result, of necessity, forms of protection developed. These protective measures are called "apotropaic spells." There were also all different types of amulets to protect oneself from curses, spells, evil spirits, and you-name-it. Amulets could be made out of anything, but precious stones and gems were considered more powerful than wood or common items.

During this time, magicians started to develop ritual tools for their magic. Some of these "magic kits" have been found at archaeological sites. Typically, they consist of a table and bowls, stones, and nails with magical inscriptions written on them.

Jesus lived in the first century during the time of the Roman occupation of Palestine. Some scholars have made the claim that the miracles of Jesus were really magic. If you strip away the theology and our modern interpretations, the miracles that Jesus performed *do* appear to be similar to what we call magic today. In fact, some of his miracles involved making a potion (Jesus spit in the mud and then applied the mud to an afflicted person's eyes to restore his sight), uttering certain words (magical incantations), and calming a storm (power over nature). He is also credited with raising the dead (Lazarus), exorcising demons, walking on water, and turning water into wine (alchemy).

If one looks at each act separately, they seem like the magical acts of a magician. Because magic was so widespread in the Roman world and used on a daily basis, even in Palestine, many people believed that Jesus was a powerful magician. As mentioned earlier, what is the difference between a miracle and magic? Isn't the distinction a theological one imposed on us in the twenty-first century?

It's my belief that Jesus was trying to restore the original use of magic. His miracles, or should we say magic, were used for good. He helped others, both physically and spiritually. Before that, magic was often used in a frivolous fashion and for selfish ends. Jesus tried to restore what magic was originally meant to be: a way to enter into the presence of God and to help us with our spiritual advancement.

I think the early Christians were aware of this. Unfortunately, as time went on, this original intention was lost. I should also point out that during the first century there were other acclaimed miracle

Figure 3.5. A Byzantine soapstone cross, eighth century CE. The five circles symbolize the five wounds of Christ. The number *five* was also considered to have metaphysical meaning in that it was often used for protection. (Note that the pentagram is a five-rayed star that is used for protection.)

Figure 3.6. A large Byzantine processional cross dating from approximately the sixth century CE. Crosses such as these were worn for protection especially by members of Christian armies. It has been broken in several places and only part of it remains.

workers besides Jesus. One such person, who many believed was as powerful as Jesus, was Apollonius of Tyana. He was credited with the ability to raise the dead and predict the future. He possessed psychic ability and could see demons. I don't know if these stories about him are true or were just made up after his death. The question arises: if they are true, was he practicing magic?

When Christianity became the state religion in 325 CE under Constantine's rule, paganism rapidly declined. Magic also started to die out, and those who continued to practice it were persecuted. The Church did a good job of almost completely annihilating its practice, especially during the Dark Ages. It was not until the Middle Ages that we see its revival; this, in my opinion, was magic's greatest hour. Angelic magic, in which angels are invoked, especially flourished at this time; it was not unusual to find Catholic priests and monks experimenting with this type of ritual magic.

The revival of magic continued into the next several centuries. One of the most important individuals of this revival was an Italian by the name of Pico della Mirandola (1463–1494). He rediscovered the Kabbalah and other esoteric teachings and published the results of his studies in Rome. In addition, a German by the name of Johannes Reuchlin (1455–1522) wrote two important works on the Kabbalah: *De Arte Cabalistica* in 1517 and *De Verbo Mirifico* in 1494. There were other revivalists, but one of the most important individuals in the revival and the spread of magic in the sixteenth century was Henry Cornelius Agrippa, on whom I have touched earlier. I will discuss Agrippa in greater detail in the next chapter.

# 4

# THE RENAISSANCE MAGICIAN— HENRY CORNELIUS AGRIPPA

The focus of this chapter is the philosophy and purpose of magic according to Henry Cornelius Agrippa. It should set the stage for the true purpose and practice of magic, which was the same for Agrippa as for Dr. John Dee, the subject of our next chapter. As mentioned earlier, Henry Cornelius Agrippa's *Three Books of Occult Philosophy,* published in 1533, is considered the bible or encyclopedia of Western magic.

I've spent a considerable amount of time studying Agrippa's life, philosophy, and works, and I believe that no one has influenced and promoted the study and practice of magic more than he.

## An Overview of the Life of Henry Cornelius Agrippa

Henricus Cornelius Agrippa von Nettesheym was born on September 14, 1496, in Cologne, Germany. His family name was Nettesheym;

Figure 4.1. Portrait of Henry Cornelius Agrippa from *The Vanity of Arts and Sciences*

the family was of the nobility and was well off. He didn't use his long last name but went by Cornelius Agrippa. Few biographies of him exist,* but it appears he was a true Renaissance man in that he had

---

*The best biography about Agrippa, in my opinion, is an out-of-print publication entitled *Agrippa and the Crisis of Renaissance Thought* by Charles G. Nauert Jr., Ph.D., who is professor emeritus at the University of Missouri. I've corresponded with Dr. Nauert and believe he is one of the world's foremost scholars on Agrippa. One of the oldest Agrippa biographies is a nineteenth-century work by Henry Morley, which has been reprinted. It's quite detailed. Unfortunately, not all the facts in it can be believed.

command of at least eight languages, was a soldier at one time, a physician, university lecturer, astrologer, alchemist, and a writer. Agrippa was even knighted on a battlefield for his bravery.*

Agrippa enrolled at the University of Cologne as a student in 1499 and graduated in 1502 with a degree of *Magister Artium* (Master of Arts). He claimed that, in addition to his master's degree, he had also earned several doctorate degrees. This has not been documented but would seem very likely due to his status and academic appointments. He claimed that the doctorates were in medicine, divinity, and law. He traveled extensively all over Europe, including the Low Countries. He was in Paris in 1507, Spain in 1508, and a soldier for several years in Italy. In 1509, he lectured at the University of Dole on the works of *De Verbo Mirifico* by John Reuchlin. This work, as previously mentioned, was significant for the revival of magic during the Renaissance.

Agrippa was accused of heresy and imprisoned several times but was never actually convicted of any crime. He was always on the move and never settled for very long in any one place. He was considered the foremost authority on the Kabbalah, magic, and esoteric subjects, and his lectures were always highly attended. During his lifetime, Agrippa published several books and many articles.

He was married three times and had a large family. Agrippa died in 1535 at the age of forty-nine in Grenoble. It's ironic that his body was buried at a Dominican monastery, the religious order that accused him of heresy and hated him the most.

---

*Agrippa could also be considered one of the world's first supporters of feminism. He strongly believed in the equality of women and advocated their rights. In 1532, he published an article entitled "The Nobility of the Female Sex and the Superiority of Women over Men."

## Agrippa's Books on Magic and Philosophy

In terms of magic, Agrippa's most significant and lasting accomplishment was the publication, in Latin, of his works on occult philosophy or magic. The first volume, *De Occulta Philosophia* (Of Occult Philosophy) was published at Antwerp in 1531. It's very likely that Agrippa himself paid for the cost of this first printing. Two years later, in 1533, all three volumes of his writings were published at Cologne under the title *De Occulta Philosophia Libri Tres* (Three Books of Occult Philosophy).

Agrippa believed that the magic being practiced in his time wasn't pure; he felt it had been corrupted over the years. He also believed that by using our minds alone we would not be able to understand or discover the mysteries of the universe and its spiritual truths and revelations. He felt that magic in its original form would give one the ability to do this. For him, magic was the highest and most sublime form of wisdom. Because he believed that much superstition had contaminated the original and true magic, restoring it to its original state was his primary aim. The end result was the *Three Books of Occult Philosophy*.

Each of the three books had their own theme. Book one was on natural magic; book two was on celestial magic; and book three was on ceremonial magic. He had written the entire work in his earlier years (approximately 1509–1510) and continued to revise and enlarge it up until it was published. (Apparently it had been circulating in an unfinished state in Europe, including the Low Countries, since 1510.)

Agrippa emphasizes that occult philosophy is indeed magic. He uses the title "Occult Philosophy" instead of the word *magic* and says that the reason he chose this title was because he didn't want to offend anyone (most likely the Church, which was fomenting the Inquisition and which he always had to stay one step ahead of). He

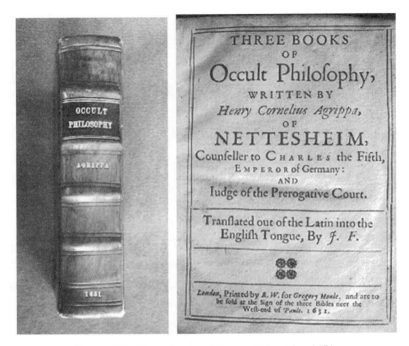

Figure 4.2. *Three Books of Occult Philosophy*, 1651,
by Henry Cornelius Agrippa

had been accused of being a sorcerer, and the publication of this book was delayed due to the efforts of the Dominican monks. This religious group seemed to be a thorn in Agrippa's side for most of his life. They eventually convinced the emperor to sentence him to death, but he fled from Germany to France to escape this fate.

The *Three Books of Occult Philosophy* was first translated into English in 1651.

This work was really an encyclopedia or compendium of almost all of the occult knowledge at that time, which Agrippa had collected from many early and ancient sources. It was not a how-to book since it didn't give directions on how to do ritual magic, but it contained all of the theory that backed up the validity of ritual magic. With a little insight and cross-referencing, one could figure out how Agrippa envisioned the rituals to be practiced. As stated earlier, after publication, it quickly became the definitive reference text for anyone wishing to practice magic, including Dr. John Dee. With its publication, information on magic was now available to people throughout Europe, and there was a tremendous surge of interest in the subject. The book was a great success, and as you might suppose, the Church was not pleased.

It's interesting to note that one of Agrippa's mentors in the study and practice of magic was an abbot at a Benedictine monastery by the name of Johannes Trithemius. Trithemius was an author who not only wrote about theology and ecclesiastical subjects but also about magic and other esoteric concerns. He was especially interested in alchemy and the philosopher's stone, which is a legendary object that can supposedly change base metal into gold. (Some believe that this stone is the Fountain of Youth and can even grant immortality.) Agrippa visited Trithemius at the Monastery of St. Jakob at Wurzburg sometime around 1509–1510 and gave him a manuscript copy of his book. Trithemius was very pleased with Agrippa and his work, and Agrippa acknowledged Trithemius at the beginning of the book.

It should be noted that in 1655 a book was published in English that claimed to be Agrippa's fourth book of occult philosophy. It appeared to be a very practical how-to book on magic and, as such, rounded out his first three books (which were conceptual in nature). This book was entitled *Henry Cornelius Agrippa His Fourth Book of Occult Philosophy, of Geomany, Magical Elements of Peter de Abano, Astronomical Gedomancy, The Nature of Spirits, Arbatel of Magic*. In fact, as you can see by the title, it was really a composite of several authors, including Peter de Abano and Geog Pictorius Villinganus. Its chapter entitled "Of Occult Philosphy or of Magical Ceremonies: The Fourth Book written by Henry Cornelius Agrippa" was mostly like written by a later author using Agrippa's name and drawing upon the information contained in his three earlier works. Most scholars believe that the chapter "of Geomany" was indeed written by Agrippa himself and that it had never been published before.

Irrespective of who wrote this fourth book, it's very valuable in that it describes how the magic that Agrippa wrote about could be practiced. (I have a facsimile edition as well as the original scans from the first English edition, and I find it to be a very interesting resource.)

Agrippa's philosophy of magic was very logical. He didn't believe the magician should be servant to or be enslaved by the higher spiritual beings (angels, demons, spirits, for example), but that these beings should render service to the magician. Thus, the magician was master, and they were the servants. An experienced and knowledgeable magician would know how to conjure up and control these forces. Also, Agrippa realized that not all the information, knowledge, and secrets of magic should be revealed to everyone but only those worthy of practicing it. He even stated that only the wise and discerning could understand and discover its true secrets; magic could be dangerous in the wrong hands, like putting dynamite into the hands of a child. Even though he realized that the magician could use magic in a selfish way, he believed it was meant to be used to discover ultimate truth and divine knowledge.

He also believed that, in the past, not all secrets and information pertaining to magic had been committed to writing but that the most important secrets had been passed orally from master to student. In addition to researching ancient books and manuscripts, he searched out the wisest and most knowledgeable magicians of his day from whom he endeavored to collect the oral traditions of magic that had been passed down to them.

Agrippa also believed that the structure of the universe was orderly and based on hierarchies or archetypes. At the top of this hierarchy is God, whose attributes are initially manifested before descending down through the lower spheres as archangels, high angels, low angels, and the lower spiritual realms, culminating in the physical realm (as discussed in chapter 1). The lower realms or worlds are reflections of the higher (as above, so below).

The following is a diagram of the hierarchy as Agrippa envisioned it:

God (chief worker)

Angels

The Heavens

The Stars

The Elements

Animals

Plants

Metals

Stones

This series of descending manifestations allows God to convey his virtues and powers upon us.

He goes on to say that there are threefold worlds: elementary (earthly or physical), celestial (related to the planets and stars), and intellectual (a spiritual world of angels and higher beings). Each specific type of magic is related to each of these worlds. His books correspond to each of these realms. Book one, on natural magic, corresponded to the elementary realm; book two, on celestial magic, concerned itself with the planets and the stars; and book three, on ceremonial magic, related to the intellectual world, which was comprised of angels and higher beings. Agrippa also emphasized that every inferior world or being is governed by its superior. He believed that, by controlling the superior, one could control the inferior, which in a sense is the basis of all magic.

Agrippa believed that both good and evil angels exist in these higher spiritual realms and that the magician can control both types. The key was to know their true names and characteristics (colors, sigils or signs, properties, etc.) in order to properly invoke and communicate with them. This is a key factor in angelic magic.

He also held that it was essential to raise the mind to the presence of God. This attitude is very important in *any* magical operation. Since God is the ultimate power, the reliance on him is of the utmost importance. Agrippa believed that the mind should be as free as possible from things of the physical world and should rise up toward God and higher spiritual thoughts. At the end of book three he states this principle:

> To conclude, in all businesses, put God before your eyes, for it's written in *Deuteronomie* When you shall seek the Lord your God, you shall find him. Whence we read in *Mark,* That whatsoever ye shall desire and pray for, believing that you shall receive it, it shal come to pas for you; . . . also the fervent prayer of a righteous man prevaileth much: . . . but take heed in your prayers, least that you should desire some vain thing, or that which is against the will of God; for God would have all things good: neither shalt thou use the name of thy God in vain, for he shall not go unpunished, who taketh his name for a vain thing: be abstemious and give alms, for the Angel saith to *Tobiah,* prayer is good with fasting and alms; and we read in the book of *Judith:* Know ye, that the Lord will hear your prayers, if ye shall persevere in fastings and prayers in his sight.[1]

There are some very important points to be learned in this statement by Agrippa, and every magician should take heed of them. As stated earlier, prayer is very important and essential to magic, and no magical operation should begin without it. Agrippa makes it very clear that God is the source of all things and everything descends from God. Without the power and presence of God, nothing will be successful or safe. A magician can perform great feats and acquire godly wisdom and knowledge if God is present with him.

Agrippa says at the beginning of the book that if you seek the Lord, you will find him. Agrippa himself gave us this important caveat: "but take heed in your prayers, least that you should desire some vain thing, or that which is against the will of God." Dr. John Dee and Agrippa agree 100 percent on this, and all magicians should follow their advice. Agrippa says that

> Magick is a faculty of wonderful virtue, full of most high mysteries, containing the most profound contemplation of most secret things, together with the nature, power, quality, substance, and virtues thereof, as also the knowledge of the whole nature, and it doth instruct us concerning the differing and agreement of things among themselves, whence it produceth its wonderful effects, by uniting the virtues of things through the application of them one to the other, and to their inferior suitable subjects, joying and knitting them together thoroughly by the powers of vertues of the superior bodies. This is the most perfect and chief Science, that sacred and sublimer kind of philosophy, and lastly the most absolute perfection of all most excellent Philosophy.[2]

This statement is a mouthful, and if you reread it carefully you will realize that Agrippa covers all the major points of magic, what it is and what it is not. This is one of the most concise and descriptive definitions of magic that I've ever read. It's also accurate in that it defines what magic, in its ideal state, should be. This is the magic that the ancients practiced and what Agrippa wanted to rediscover for his time.

I would like to take some of the points above about magic that Agrippa mentions and list them below. I've modernized the English and made the phrases more concise.

Magic:

- is full of wonderful virtues
- is full of most high mysteries
- contains the most profound contemplation of most secret things
- produces wonderful effects
- unites the virtues of things
- is the most perfect and chief science

Figure 4.3. Eighteenth-century sealed relic, which has never been opened. It might likely contain a piece of the true cross or a fragment of a saint's bone.

- contains sacred and sublime philosophy
- is the most absolute perfection of all the most excellent philosophy

This is the type of magic that God and the angels originally gave humanity, and it is the magic of the ancients. This is the type of magic that Agrippa wanted to restore and bring back to the world. Did Agrippa actually experience these spiritual and sublime states using magic? We know he mentioned to a close friend that he never enjoyed the mystical experience of oneness or union with God that he sought, but perhaps he experienced it later in his life. Unfortunately, unless new information comes to light, we will never know. What's important to acknowledge is that, although Agrippa may never have had this kind of experience for himself, he believed that human beings were entitled to it and should make the achievement of it a focus of their lives.

It's interesting that in today's world one has to be a specialist in a certain field in order to "make it." However, no one person can be an expert in everything. Yet Agrippa argued that the opposite was true. He told people that it was more important to have a general knowledge of *all* things rather than to concentrate on just one area. This represents the idea of the Renaissance man who manifested many talents—that of artist, scientist, or philosopher or several of these, for instance.

Agrippa also strongly urged his students to read and study the Bible. He believed it was essential to make this a priority. It's significant that he wrote a paper defending the proper veneration of the relics of saints. (Please see plate 8 of the color insert for a collection of relics.)

There appears to be one inconsistency in Agrippa's life, which I would like to discuss briefly. In 1531 he published a book entitled *De incertitudine et vanitate scientiarum et artium, atque excellentia verbi Dei declamation* [*The Vanity of Arts and Sciences*], in which he appeared to retract his book on occult philosophy. (Please see plate 9 of the color insert.)

There are several possibilities as to why he did this. He knew he was being watched by agents of the Inquisition, and perhaps this was a ploy to get them off his back. If arrested, he could say he had recanted his work. On the other hand, I believe there is no real inconsistency between these two works. He believed in the reality of magic, and he was alluding to that by saying, in *The Vanity of Arts and Sciences,* that the only acceptable use of magic is to find God. Everything else is vanity.

This will be debated for centuries, but I believe my explanation is reasonable. Agrippa was a Christian and was always very careful in stating that it was wrong to get involved with demons or evil spirits. His use of magic was always for the highest purposes. He stated that a person practicing magic must have faith and a proper attitude toward God. He also said what everyone has been saying for centuries: Magic can be used for good or evil, and a person's belief and faith in God will keep him or her from going in the direction of evil. The attitude, belief, and viewpoint of the magician are important factors in keeping him safe from harm:

> . . . for holy Religion purges the mind and makes it Divine, it helps nature, and strengthens natural powers, as a Physician helps the healing of the body and a Husbandman the strength of the earth. Whosoever therefore, Religion being laid aside, do confide only in natural things are likely often to be deceived by evil spirits; but from the knowledge of Religion, the contempt and cure of vices arises, and a safeguard against evil spirits. . . .[3]*

As we know, God told Solomon that he could ask for anything, and it would be given to him. Solomon asked for wisdom:

> In that night God appeared to Solomon, and said to him, "Ask what I shall give you." And Solomon said to God, "You have shown great and steadfast love to David my father, and have made me king in his place. O Lord God, let your word to David my father be now fulfilled, for you have made me king over a people as numerous as the dust of the earth. Give me now wisdom and knowledge to go out and come in before this people, for who can govern this people of yours, which is so great?" God answered Solomon, "Because this was in your heart, and you have not asked possessions, wealth, honor, or the life of those who hate you, and have not even asked long life, but have asked wisdom and knowledge for yourself that you may govern my people over whom I've made you king, wisdom and knowledge are granted to you. I will also give you riches, possessions, and honor, such as none of the kings had who were before you, and none after you shall have the like." So Solomon came from the high place

---

*I've edited this quote for easy reading.

at Gibeon, from before the tent of meeting, to Jerusalem. And he reigned over Israel.

2 CHRONICLES 1:7–13

I hope we all have the spiritual discernment to ask for wisdom also. You can see how different this approach is to magic than what we saw of the practice of magic in the cultures of the Egyptians, the Mesopotamians, the Greeks, and the Romans. Magic had certainly degenerated from its true purpose, and you can see why Agrippa wanted to restore it to its original purity and spiritual essence. This was a mighty task. It was not finished by him but by Dr. John Dee years later. Dr. Dee, through his angelic communications, brought a specific practice to the world.

# 5

# HE SPOKE TO ANGELS—
# THE LIFE OF DR. JOHN DEE

*He had a very fair, clear complexione; a long beard as white
as milke. A very handsome man. . . . He was a great peace-
maker. . . . He was tall and slender. He wore a gowne like
artist's gowne, wit hanging sleeves, and a slitt. A might
good man he was.*

A DESCRIPTION OF JOHN DEE FROM
*BRIEF LIVES, CHIEFLY OF CONTEMPORARIES,
SET DOWN BY JOHN AUBREY, BETWEEN
THE YEARS 1699 AND 1696*

The magic that I will be teaching you is based on the angelic communications of Dr. John Dee. It's not the type in which angels and demons
are summoned, controlled, and used to carry out your bidding, but the
type in which you enter higher spiritual realms or dimensions (called
Aethyrs or Heavens) and communicate with the good resident angels
in each realm. Dr. Dee's sole purpose in contacting the angels was for
spiritual knowledge, enlightenment, and wisdom.

I always liked the name Dr. John Dee because it is so similar to
mine. When I was a professor, "Dr. D." is what my students usually

called me. John Dee was born in London on July 13, 1527. His father, Rowland Dee, held an appointment at the court, and his mother, Johanna Wilde Dee, was descended from nobility. It's interesting that Nostradamus also lived at this time (1503–1566). It's not known if he and Dee ever met.

Figure 5.1. A portrait of Dr. John Dee

As a child, Dee attended the Chantry School at Chelmsford and was well educated in mathematics, grammar, and Latin. He eventually matriculated to St. John's College at Cambridge in 1542 at the age of fifteen, from which he graduated in 1545 with a bachelor's degree. At the close of the same year, he was selected as one of the original fellows at Trinity College and also appointed "Under-Reader" in Greek. He became a skillful astronomer, taking "thousands of observations of the heavenly influences and operations" and published this information in an ephemeris. He stated that, while at college, he only got about four hours of sleep a night, due to his persistent studying.

There is a very interesting story about him while he was a student at Cambridge. He was involved in a Greek play, the *Pax* by Aristophanes. He used his skills and ingenuity to build a large mechanical beetle, which gave the actual impression that it could fly with a person sitting on top of it. These theatrics had never been seen before, and they stunned the audience who couldn't believe that the beetle's flight was accomplished solely by physical means. They felt that some supernatural method, in other words, magic, must have been involved. From this time on, many viewed Dr. Dee as a sorcerer; this label stayed with him the rest of his life.

Dee left England for the first time in 1547 to meet with scholars and professors of science and mathematics at Dutch universities. He also spent several months in the Low Countries meeting with famous individuals, including Gerard Mercator, Gemma Frisius, Joannes Caspar Myricaeus, Antonius Gogava, and other well-known scientists, inventors, and scholars. When he returned to England, he brought with him two great globes manufactured by Mercator and some newly invented astronomical apparatuses. Dee entered Cambridge to study for his master's degree, and in 1548 he left for the University of Louvain in Belgium to continue his studies, for which many believe he was awarded a doctorate degree. He was extremely popular in Paris, and the frequent lectures he gave were standing room only. He returned to England in 1551 and authored several papers.

Mary Tudor (universally known as Bloody Mary) ascended the throne in 1553 and became Queen Mary. Several years later, in 1555, Dee was arrested on charges of conjuring spirits and heresy. Fortunately, he only served a few months in prison; the charges were dropped and he was exonerated. He soon began a friendship and correspondence with Princess Elizabeth and also cast her horoscope. When Princess Elizabeth became queen in 1558, she asked Dee to calculate the most propitious date for her coronation. He had become her most trusted adviser.

One of Dee's visions was to create a state library of books and manuscripts. He presented a proposal to the queen entitled *A Supplication for the recovery and preservation of ancient writers and monuments*. Unfortunately, nothing came of Dee's proposal, so he decided to continue to collect and expand his own large library of books and manuscripts until it was one of the largest private libraries in Europe. It was estimated that Dee's library contained over four thousand volumes.

Another interesting story concerning Dee involves an accusation of him practicing magic. A wax image of the queen with a pin stuck through it was discovered lying in a field. The entire court was up in arms and believed someone had done this to cast a death spell on the queen. Dee was summoned immediately by Elizabeth and the court. He convinced them he had nothing to do with the incident and that it was probably just some practical joke. He allayed their fears and they accepted his explanation. This is a good example of how Dee was respected by the queen and how she valued him; she kept him close for this reason.

The queen referred to Dr. Dee as "her eyes," and some speculate that in his travels all over Europe, he may have acted as a spy for her. He was one of the top cryptographers of the time, and it would have been natural for him to spy on other countries and send cryptic messages back to the court and the queen. As pointed out by Richard Deacon in his book *John Dee, Scientist, Geographer, Astrologer, and Secret Agent to*

*Elizabeth I,* in their private correspondence, Dee signed his name with two circles representing his eyes and a sideways upside-down elongated seven. (Was Dee 007 the first James Bond?!)

In 1558, Dr. Dee authored a book on astronomy entitled *Propaedeumata Aphoristica.* It was a sophisticated approach to astronomy, integrating several fields of study including geometry and mathematics. In 1563, he traveled to Switzerland, Hungary, Italy, and Antwerp to visit universities and other scholars.

Dr. Dee was a very prolific writer and an expert on almost every major area of the arts and sciences. He was considered England's greatest and most famous scholar whom many other scholars from all over Europe visited; to them, he availed his great library of rare books and manuscripts. He also received many invitations from different emperors to stay in their country and be well supported, but he declined these because he didn't want to leave his beloved England.

Dee is noted for advancing the fields of mathematics, cartography, navigation, cryptology, astronomy, and medicine, as well as many others. He is probably most famous for writing the preface for the first English edition of *Euclid's Elements of Geometry* (1570). In this introduction, which is quite lengthy, he attempted to show that the sciences, theology, and philosophy are all related and that their unifying factors are mathematics and geometry. Instead of trying to separate each category of learning, as many did at the time, Dr. Dee attempted to integrate them into a whole.

He also gave many illuminating lectures on Euclid's geometry at universities all over Europe. Some attribute the revival of mathematics during the Renaissance to him. He also played a major role in the scientific revolution of that time, training many famous English explorers in navigation and cartography with his own state-of-the-art navigational equipment. Many explorers came to him for lessons in the use of his navigational equipment, and in 1577, he published *General and Rare Memorials Pertaining to the Perfect Art of Navigation.* He also coined the term *British Empire* and advocated the expansion of the kingdom.

Dee was very much interested in the calendar and wrote a detailed paper on reforming the Gregorian calendar.

Dee eventually moved to his mother's house at Mortlake on the Thames. He expanded the home so it could house his large library, laboratories, workers, and servants. His first book was published in 1564 and was entitled the *Monas Hieroglyphica*. It was a very odd combination of mathematics, geometry, the Kabbalah, and alchemy— full of occult symbols and mathematical relationships between these strange figures. Very few have understood it. In fact, Dee himself hinted that a key was needed to unravel its mysteries. What this key is remains unknown. Dee claimed that he wrote and completed this work in thirteen days in January of 1564. I believe it would be impossible to complete this work in such a short amount of time. My speculation is that Dee may have executed this work by automatic writing or had help from some spiritual source. If and when the key to this work is discovered, I believe wonderful secrets and mysteries will be revealed.

Dee was married three times. His first wife, Katherine Constable, whom he married in 1565, died in 1574. He was married a second time in 1575 to a woman whose name has not come down to us; she died the following year. He and his third wife, Jane Fromond, were married in 1578. She gave him at least eight children (some say nine or ten). She died of the plague in 1605, only three years before Dee's death. Dee actually named one of his daughters, Madami, after the name of one of the angels he was communicating with. This demonstrated his belief and respect for the angels. (What father would name his daughter after something that was not good and loving?)

## Dr. Dee's Later Years

After Dee turned fifty, he started to spend more time studying and researching the occult and developed an obsession with contacting the angels. Like Agrippa, he believed that one couldn't find the answers to the highest mysteries through academic learning but only by spiritual experience and contact with higher spiritual beings.

Dee's most cherished book was Agrippa's *Three Books on Occult Philosophy* that, as I stated previously, he always kept near him during any magical operation. In fact, he had several copies of Agrippa's book in Latin, which were the editions published in 1531 and 1533. I believe these Latin versions served as his manuals for angelic communications, at least during his initial experiments in trying to contact the angels. Unfortunately, he had little success with these early efforts.

Also, as he admitted, he was not very good at scrying. He does record in his diary two successful attempts at this, however. One occurred in May of 1581 in which he saw an angel in one of his crystals. Then, in November of 1582, he saw the angel Uriel who gave him a crystal and told him this would help him see the spirits and angels of the heavenly realms. Dee had hired several different scryers, who he believed had the gift; they tried to contact the angels for him. He was not really satisfied with any of them until he met Edward Kelley (formerly Edward Talbot?) in 1582. Kelley was born in 1555 and died in 1595.

Kelley was an interesting character. Rumor had it that part of one or both ears had been cut off as a punishment for counterfeiting coins. He may have also changed his name from Kelly to Talbot at one time, but no one is certain of this. He was mainly interested in alchemy, not angelic communications, and in fact, he wrote on this subject. Kelley's motivation in meeting Dee was to consult with him on his alchemical experiments, in which he was attempting to transform base metals into silver and gold. Dee was not interested in alchemy at that time but, wanting to pursue angelic communications, he needed a talented and gifted scryer. Kelley definitely had the gift for scrying, and he and Dee soon became successful at invoking and communicating with the angels. Kelley's tool was a quartz crystal ball; Kelley could clairvoyantly both see and hear the angels in the crystal.

Plate 1. A very rare hand-colored plate from Raphael's *Familiar Astrology*, which was published in 1849. This book is a composite of many articles on astrology, magic, alchemy, and divination. Its caption, stating that millions of spiritual creatures walk the earth unseen, illustrates the principle of magic.

Plate 2. Another rare plate from Raphael's *Familiar Astrology* illustrates the stereotypical magician conjuring up spirits, entities, and beings.

Plate 3. In the Catholic Church, the Exposition of the Blessed Sacrament resembles a drawing from ancient Egypt showing the priests worshiping the sun god. The sun god in the illustration looks exactly like a monstrance (the stand holding the host) used in the Exposition of the Blessed Sacrament. (From *The Two Babylons* by Alexander Hislop)

Plate 4. Crystal balls are the most common object used for scrying. Dr. John Dee had a crystal ball about the size of this one, which is two inches in diameter. It was placed on his magic table and Edward Kelley used it for scrying.

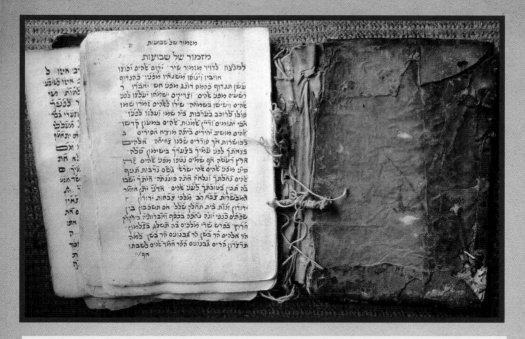

Plate 5. The remains of an ancient Hebrew prayer book. Notice there are additional leaves sewn into the covers.

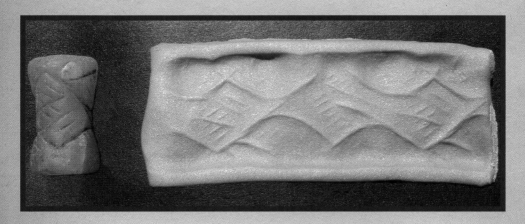

Plate 6. An ancient cylinder seal (left), dated to approximately 3000 BCE, with magical patterns. It's very rare in that it was made with quartz crystal, which was typical of seals that were used as a talisman or for magic. They were rolled onto clay to produce a pattern like the one shown here at right.

Plate 7. A very early Christian ring with the IC XC and two letters, one above and one below, which was probably an abbreviation for a magical inscription used for the protection of the wearer. It dates back to approximately 400–500 CE. The stone is a bloodstone, symbolizing the crucifixion of Christ; when he was dying, his blood dripped on a stone and it became a bloodstone.

Plate 8. A collection of first-class relics (containing a body part such as a bone or some hair) of different saints

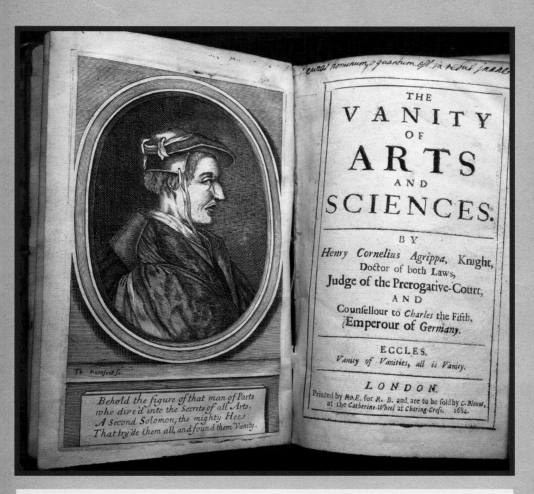

Plate 9. The title page of *The Vanity of Arts and Sciences* by Henry Cornelius Agrippa

Plate 10 (opposite). The author John DeSalvo holding a copy of a scan from one of the pages of the tables from the Book of Enoch. The original tables are in the British Library; this copy is used with their permission.

Plate 11. Enochian is read from right to left like Hebrew. In this illustration, reading from right to left gives you the name BAPPOMGEL.

Plate 12. These objects were re-created from ancient drawings showing the Egyptian rods that the Pharaohs held. Their purpose was to balance the body and spirit.

Plate 13 (left). A large crystal from the altar of the late Nick Nocerino, one of the leading researchers and authorities on crystal skulls. It is thought that holding crystals in your hands helps to balance the energies of the body.

Plate 14 (below). Crystal skulls have also been used for scrying. This crystal skull was given to the author by the late Nick Nocerino, founder of the Society of Crystal Skulls, who believed that crystal skulls are intricate computers that can be activated by the use of color and sound.

Dee and Kelley were invited to Poland by the Polish prince Albertus Laski, who had a keen interest in their angelic communications. Dee, Kelley, and their families left for Poland in 1583. While there, some of the more important angelic information was received by Kelley and Dee. After leaving Poland, they traveled the continent, eventually returning to England in 1589. It was very unfortunate that just after Dee left for Poland, a mob—who obviously didn't like him and believed he was a sorcerer—broke into his home and destroyed his scientific equipment and many of his rare books and manuscripts.

During his lifetime, Dr. Dee had constant skirmishes with the Church and its high-ranking officials because of his spiritual beliefs. It's a shame that whenever a new idea is put forth that upsets the status quo, there is persecution of the originator. Even today, if new research or discoveries conflict with the currently accepted ideas in academia, the innovator becomes an outcast and is subject to humiliation.

It was no different in Dee's time; back then you could lose your life as a result of the Inquisition. Some readers may be familiar with *Foxe's Book of Martyrs,* which is John Foxe's (1517–1587) detailed survey of the history of Christian martyrs. This book highlights the sufferings and torture of the English Protestants under Queen Mary. The first edition was published in 1563, and there were several later editions. Dee is mentioned in the book as a great conjurer. Most churches had copies of this book, and it must have really bothered Dee to be slandered all across the country. He protested to Foxe, and in the 1567 printing, all mention of him was removed from the book. Even though Dee was successful in purging his name, however, the damage had been done, and he was still labeled a conjurer by most of the general public. This may have led him to do something drastic, as I will soon discuss.

In 1595, Edward Kelley died, and Dee lost his colleague and closest friend. Kelley had been living in Prague and conducting alchemical experiments for Emperor Rudolph. It appears that Kelley had never succeeded in transmuting base metal into gold, and the emperor finally lost

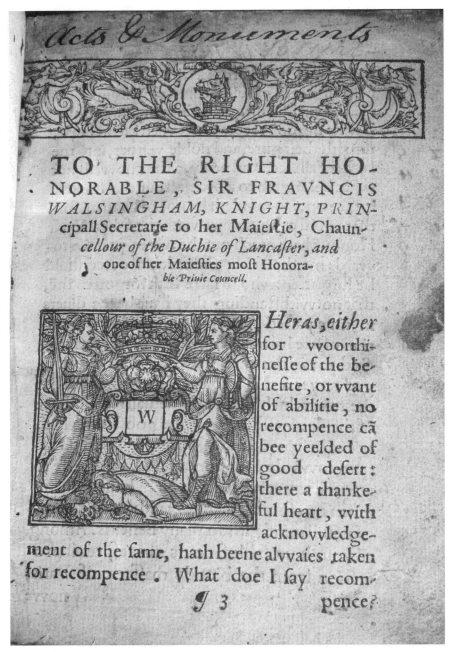

Figure 5.2. The title page from the 1589 edition of *Foxe's Book of Martyrs*

patience with him and threw him into prison in a castle. He died while attempting to escape the castle.

Dee's other most intimate friend, Queen Elizabeth, died in 1603. When she passed away, Dee lost the one person who had always protected him from bogus accusations of heresy and sorcery. It's important to note that she was not only a queen and benefactor to Dee, but a close personal friend as well. I'm sure her death was a terrible blow to him and hard for him to overcome. He now was seventy-six years old and alone, with no protectorate and many enemies who were willing to falsely accuse him. Adding to this, King James, who succeeded Elizabeth, seemed to take a more aggressive and serious view of witchcraft and sorcery. James was the author of three books on demonology, which was about witches who had confessed to the crime of witchcraft. These volumes eventually became an important reference book for witch hunters. James was a believer in the ability of witches to summon the devil and make pacts with him.

When Parliament met in 1604 during James' first year as king, he urged its members to enact new and more stringent laws banning witchcraft. This recommendation was referred to the bishops, who modified and edited it before approving it later that year.

Dee decided to go on the offensive. On June 5, 1604, he petitioned King James in the strongest of terms

> to cause your Highnesses said servant (John Dee) to be tried and cleared of that horrible and damnable, and to him most grievous and damageable slander, generally, and for these many years last past, in this kingdom raised and continued, by report and print against him, namely that he is or hath bin a conjurer or caller or invocator of devils.

He explained that he had previously published his arguments against such accusations and that should have rested his case. He was now offering himself to be tried under penalty of death. In his own words:

yea eyther to be stoned to death, or to be buried quicke, or to be
burned unmercifully, if by any due, true, and just meanes, the name
of conjuror, or caller, or invocator of Divels or damned Sprites, can
be proved to have beene or to be duely or justly reported and told of
him (as to have been of his doing) were true, as they have been told
or reasonably caused any wondering among or to the many-headed
multitude, or to any other whoseever else.

He ends his petition with "a great and undoubted hope" that the
king will "soon redress his farder griefs and hindrances, no longer of
him possibly to be endured, so long hath his utter undoing, by little and
little, beene most unjustly compassed."[1]

Unfortunately, or perhaps fortunately for him, parliament ignored
his petition. They must have felt that this old man, who had been
harassed so much in his life, was harmless and posed no real threat
to the kingdom. King James also ignored his request, and never again
was Dee accused of heresy. He lived out the rest of his life in poverty,
attended only by his daughter Katherine. He expected to receive money
for some previous appointments, but this money never materialized. He
even attempted, during his last years, to find buried treasure, possibly
by using angelic communication or other means. He paid his expenses
by selling rare books from his library, and this must have broken his
heart.

He died at Mortlake on March 26, 1609, and was buried at the
Church of St. Mary the Virgin. Shakespeare kept the name of Dee alive
by writing Dee into his play *The Tempest* as the magician Prospero.
This play was first performed in 1611, two years after Dee's death. His
life seems to have been similar to the lives of so many others who are
ahead of their time.

The following is excerpted from Dee's letter to the Archbishop of
Canterbury, written in approximately 1594 but not published until
1604, in which he defends his study of magic and other subjects:

Before the Almighty our GOD, and your Lordships good Grace . . . that with all my heart, with all my soul; with all my strength, power and understanding (according to the measure thereof, which the Almighty hath given me) for the most part of the time, from my youth hitherto, I've used and still use, good, lawful, honest, Christian and divinely prescribed means to attain to the knowledge of those truths, which are meet, and necessary for me to know; and where- with to do his divine Majesty such service, as he hath, doth, and will call me unto, during this my life: for his honor and glory advancing, and for the benefit, and commoditie publique of this Kingdome; so much, as by the will and purpose of God, shall lie in my skill, and ability to perform: as a true, faithful, and most sincerely dutifully servant, to our most gracious and incomparable Queen Elizabeth, and as a very comfortable fellow-member of the body politique, gov- erned under the scepter Royal of our earthly Supreme head (Queen Elizabeth) and as a lively sympathicall, and true symetricall fellow member of that holy and mystical body, Catholiquely extended and placed (wheresoever) on the earth: in the view, Knowledge, direc- tion, protection, illumination and consolation of the Almighty, most Blessed, most holy, most glorious, comajesticall, coeternall, and coes- sentiall Trinity: The Head of that Body, being only our Redeemer, Christ Jesus, perfect God, and perfect man. . . .[2]

Dee really tried to make the point that everything he had accom- plished, written, and taught was done as a result of his faith in God, Jesus Christ, and the Church. He is adamant about this and leaves no stone unturned in his plea. I don't believe that Dee wrote this to escape the Inquisition. Nor was it just a political ploy; he had already offered himself to be tried by King James. This is consistent with his view of magic. Magic is of God, of Jesus Christ, and is aligned with the teachings of the Church. Dee always believed this and never for one moment in his life thought that he was doing anything that had not been ordained by God. We will also see in the next several chapters that his angelic magic is consistent with his statement quoted above.

I would like to speculate about an aspect of Dee's life that, as far as I know, no one has addressed. I mentioned that, during his last years, he attempted to find buried treasure using angelic communications or other means. The question arises: what could these other means be? I don't think Dee would have used the angels to help him find buried treasure because he would have felt that these angelic communications were of God and very holy. To use them for such a selfish and materialistic purpose would be wrong. I really think he would have looked for another method. That's my opinion, and the more one reads about Dee and studies his life, the more sense this makes.

What could these other means for finding buried treasure have been? Given that Dee experimented with many occult techniques of the time, it's highly probable that he may have been a practitioner of dowsing.

Many people think of dowsing as a method of locating underground water, but it's actually a type of divination, during which the dowser uses a device like a stick or a swinging pendulum to locate underground water, minerals, or treasure. Some think it works through some unconscious force. Others think it works by psychic force, either from spirits,

Figure 5.3. An ancient Egyptian alabaster papyrus amulet (1500 BCE)
that may have been used for dowsing or divination

angels, or some unknown energy. Whether you believe in the power of dowsing or not, there is compelling evidence to show that some people do have a gift for this type of divination. Would Dee have used this method of divination to try to find buried treasure? Even though I don't have definitive proof, I believe the answer is yes.

I didn't realize that one of my heroes, Albert Einstein, was interested in dowsing and experimented with it, even though he believed it had a natural explanation. Here is an excerpt from one of his letters dated February 15, 1946:

> I know very well that many scientists consider dowsing as they do astrology, as a type of ancient superstition. According to my conviction this is, however, unjustified. The dowsing rod is a simple instrument that shows the reaction of the human nervous system to certain factors which are unknown to us at this time.[3]

## The Importance of Spiritual Protection

Discussing pendulum divination gives me the opportunity to broach something very important that anyone who does any occult practices, including magic, should be aware of: people doing occult practices always need to protect themselves from negative energies and beings. Once you open yourself up to the spiritual world and are unprotected, you could come under attack by these negative influences. Protection is of the utmost importance. In the chapter that presents instructions for Enochian Meditation, I will be teaching you one of the oldest and most powerful forms of magical protection. It's called the Lesser Banishing Ritual of the Pentagram (LBRP) and only takes a few minutes to do.

Protecting yourself from negative influences is necessary whether you're performing ritual magic, or using a pendulum for divination, or are involved in ghost hunting. I was not aware of the need for this precaution until I conferred with some well-known ghost hunters. I had been experimenting with electronic voice phenomena (EVPs), that is, trying to record the voices of ghosts on digital recorders. I achieved some results at first, but I felt like I was leaving myself open to unwanted energies. When I consulted with my ghost-hunting friends, they told me to always employ spiritual protection when involved in any type of paranormal research, from ghost hunting to spiritualism to magic.

They explained that members of their team always protect themselves whenever they go to any haunted place to do their work. One of the team members told me that she visualizes a white light around her. (I will be teaching this technique to you later.) I now personally use both the White Light Visualization and the LBRP together. As a result, I feel that I have added protection and never worry about negative entities or influences. I always perform these types of protection before and after any occult techniques or experiments.

We don't have any indication from Dee's diaries that he used any special form of protection such as the LBRP or the White Light Visualization. There is also no indication that he used the "License to Depart"—words that are said aloud to make sure all the spirits leave at the end of a session. (This is also covered later in this book.) What he did do was recite very long and intense prayers, especially a recitation of the psalms and prayers to God. I feel that this was just as good in that he called on the powers of God and the good angels to protect him.

The method of protection you use is up to you, but I still strongly recommend the LBRP for whatever occult practice you do. The LBRP is so ancient that we don't even know where and when it originated. It's commonly used by most magicians today to open and close all magical ceremonies. Even if I'm not performing any magic rituals, I try to do the LBRP on a daily basis to purify and cleanse my atmosphere.

## An Intriguing Discovery

I will end this chapter with one of my favorite stories regarding the preservation of Dee's manuscripts. Fortunately, since Dee took copious notes and keep several diaries, we have much original source material from his own pen. A fascinating story is how, fifty-four years after he died, some unknown manuscripts of his were discovered. Some time after his death, furniture from his home at Mortlake was sold. Over the years, these items made their rounds from one owner to another. (I doubt the owners knew that it was the furniture of the famous Dr. Dee.) A most interesting piece, a wood chest measuring about four-and-a-half-feet long, would had have several different owners until something extraordinary was discovered about it by its last owners, Robert and Susannah Jones. They bought the Dee chest in approximately 1643, and it remained with them for the next twenty years. In or about 1662, they decided to move the chest to a new place in their home, and when picking it up and moving it, they heard something rattle inside.

Robert Jones explored the bottom of the chest with a piece of iron and found a crevice that opened up to a secret compartment. Inside this secret drawer were unknown manuscripts of Dr. Dee and a rosary chaplet made of olive wood. Unfortunately, the Jones didn't realize the significance of what they had found, and the maid used some of the manuscript to wrap pies in and light fires with. (I shudder to think how many manuscripts were destroyed by the Jones' maid. Some have estimated that a half-dozen manuscripts of Dee's were lost to the world forever.) Robert and Susannah eventually realized that the remaining manuscripts in their possession might be valuable and removed them to a place of safekeeping.

Several years later, Robert died and Susannah married Thomas Wale, who was a good friend of the well-known antiquarian scholar and book collector, Elias Ashmole. (Ashmole was also a Freemason and very interested in the occult and metaphysics.) Robert decided to show

Ashmole the papers. Ashmole realized their importance at once and obtained them from Robert, eventually passing them on to the British Library. (Ashmole's antiquarian collection, in fact, makes up a significant part of the British Library today.) Due to Ashmole's insight and generosity, we now are privy to these previously unknown manuscripts of Dr. John Dee, which are highly significant to the world of magic and may otherwise have been lost to the world.

I would like to briefly comment on some of the specific manuscripts found in the chest. The first four contain Dee's angelic magic system and were published by Robert Turner in 1986 and 1989. The last one, *The Five Books of Mystery,* comprises Dr. Dee's spiritual diaries from the years 1581 to 1583. It was published by Joseph H. Peterson in 2003. The manuscripts found in the chest include:

1. Forty-eight *Claves Angelicae* (Forty-eight Angelic Keys)
2. *Liber Scientiae Auxilii et Victoriae Terrestris* (The Book of Knowledge, Help, and Earthly Victory)
3. A Book of Invocations
4. *De Heptarchia Mystica* (The Mysteries of the Sevenfold Kingdom)
5. *Mysteriorum Libri Quinque* (Five Books of Mystery)

The first book of Dr. Dee's, "The Forty-eight Keys or Calls," is the one I will be focusing on and developing our Enochian Meditation from. It consists of basic invocations dictated in the Enochian language to Dee and Kelley by the angels. The angels also gave them the English translation for each Call.

The second book, "The Book of Knowledge, Help, and Earthly Victory," contains a set of tables that give information related to the last thirty of the forty-eight Angelic Calls (the Calls of the Thirty Aethyrs). It gives the name of each Aethyr, the names of the governors (angels) of each Aethyr, the parts of the earth associated with each one, the symbol or sigils associated with each governor, and the ruling kings and tribes of Israel of each area.

The third book, "A Book of Invocations," written in Latin, is comprised of invocations for the angels who rule over the four quarters of the earth. The angels' names are derived from a table composed of squares with a letter in each one.

The fourth book, "The Mysteries of the Sevenfold Kingdom," is basically planetary invocations of good angels. There are a total of forty-nine angels (seven Kings, seven Princes, and thirty-five lesser angels), which are placed in a table called *Tabula Angelorum Bonorum 49* (The Table of Forty-nine Good Angels).

The fifth book, "Five Books of Mystery," contained Dee's spiritual diaries from March 1582 to May 1583 and documented his first angelic communications during that time.

Dee received much information from the angels, but did he not receive instructions on how to use or apply the information. We will only be using the last thirty of the forty-eight Angelic Calls (the Calls of the Thirty Aethyrs) for our Enochian Meditation.

# 6

# THE ANGELIC MAGIC
# OF DR. DEE

I would now like to address the type of magic that Dr. Dee was given by the angels and the specific type that you will be practicing. As discussed earlier, some types of Enochian Magic allow one to summon specific angels and demons. I believe this type of magic has risks and dangers and isn't always a path toward God. I will not be teaching this form of magic but rather the Enochian Magic, which allows one to move toward God and enter higher spiritual dimensions.

Why was this information (about evil angels) given to Dee from the angels in the first place, and did he believe it was permissible for a magician—at certain times or under certain circumstances—to conjure up evil spirits? These questions don't have a simple answer. In general, it's apparent that Dr. Dee only attempted to contact and communicate with the good angels. This can be seen and illustrated in his angelic communications, in which he questions the angels to determine if they are from God and also tests them to see if they are evil. Whenever evil spirits show up, he is quick to identify them and attempts to get rid of them expeditiously.

He also is very hard on Edward Kelley when he suspects that Kelley had been practicing some form of black magic on the side. (The angels also chastised Kelley for this.) In Dee's diaries, there are no indications that he wanted to conjure up or communicate with evil angels; this would go against his entire philosophy. He was a very pious and spiritual man, and his entire purpose for communicating with the angels was to obtain the wisdom and knowledge of God and understand spiritual mysteries.*

The most important question is: why did the angels give this information to Dr. Dee and thus to the world? To be honest, I don't know, but I *can* speculate. I believe the angels have an obligation to reveal *all* available information pertaining to a spiritual revelation or spiritual communication. They don't have the authority to decide what to give and what not to give. We have free will, which we can use to make choices about what to do with what we're given.

Perhaps the answer to this question is that all religious and sacred writings seem to tell the same story: with the sacred information given, human beings, with their free will, can either move toward the light or to the dark side; they can use this information for good or for ill.

I'd like to make an important point about the actual practice of magic, which is sometimes overlooked. For a novice, it might appear that the instructions and procedures for carrying out a ritual are very specific, almost like a cookbook recipe. This observation is essentially correct and seems to place magic in the category of science. It's not unlike a chemical experiment in that you obtain specific chemicals, mix measured amounts of them together, heat them up, distill them, and then separate the products. This may seem to make magic a dry procedure for the beginner, but that's only half of the story because, in actual fact, magic is both a science and an *art*.

For any type of new practice, you need a basic framework to start with; otherwise there would be no order, and chaos would ensue. But just because you initially have a framework doesn't mean you always need

---

*We have to be very thankful to Dee for keeping such good notes. In fact, he kept several diaries, one for his magical works and one for his daily life. It's amusing that in his daily diary, he would make a note (a cryptic symbol) when he had intercourse with his wife! I'm sure he would have been shocked to think that some four hundred years later, when his diaries were published, the entire world would know about his sex life because someone had figured out what that symbol meant!

to stay within it. You can improvise and improve on the basic structure of your ritual as time goes on. This creative improvisation constitutes the artful half of the creation of magic. To be a successful magician you need creativity, intuition, and the drive to explore new frontiers. As an artist, your canvas is the spiritual realm.

I always suggest that, at the beginning of your work, you stay within the basic framework until you learn the ritual by heart and feel comfortable with it. That's standard advice for learning any new system, and that's exactly what Dr. Dee did. His framework or standard was Agrippa's *Three Books of Occult Philosophy*. He followed Agrippa's rules and procedures until he made contact with the angels, and then it was a whole new ballgame. The angels instructed him how to stay in contact with them, and they also told him what they wanted him to do in order to be able to receive the Enochian language and the Calls for the Aethyrs from them.

The Calls that they gave Dee and Kelley were invocations that, if repeated, would act like keys to open up specific Aethyrs or heavenly realms. Once an Aethyr was entered, its resident angel could be contacted. Dee and Kelley were given the specific Calls for each of the Aethyrs and the names of the resident angels of each. What's strange is that the angels explained very little in the way of details about the actual procedures for *using* the Calls. They only told Dee and Kelley that the Calls opened up the Aethyrs or Heavens.

Why give this information and not give detailed explanations? Maybe *we* need to work out the details and applications for ourselves. Maybe this information was only to be used in the future by someone who could figure out how to apply it in a specific way. Maybe the information would be given later, but Dee and Kelley broke off the angelic communications before it could be given. We can speculate all we want to, but at the end of the day, we don't have a definitive answer. That's why, based on Dee's information, so many different procedures by so many different magical groups have been developed.

The important point here is that there is more to be discovered and unveiled in the magic that Dee was given, especially with regard to how to use the Enochian Calls. I believe that this information remains hidden in Dee's diaries. What's important to remember also is that we don't possess *all* of Dr. Dee's diaries. We know for a fact that some were destroyed, some may have been lost, and some may still be hidden.

Maybe someone in our own time will unveil or discover the information that Dee was not yet aware of. *You* can explore these hidden spiritual realities, invoke the angels of the Atheyrs, and perhaps discover some hidden secrets yourself! This is a very real option for anyone embarking on the practice of Enochian Magic.

## What the Angels Told Dee

We know that the angels told Dr. John Dee that the information they were conveying to him was the information or magical workings that God had previously given to the famous Enoch of the Bible. The Bible says that Enoch never died but was taken up to heaven by God:

> When Enoch had lived 65 years, he fathered Methuselah. Enoch walked with God after he fathered Methuselah 300 years and had other sons and daughters. Thus all the days of Enoch were 365 years. Enoch walked with God, and he was not, for God took him.
>
> Genesis 5:21–24

The angels told Dee that this language was also the language that Adam and Eve had been given by the angels. This would have been the original language of humankind, which named everything by its true name or essence. As we have learned, to know the true name of something was to give one power over it. Given this, we can understand why Dee was so excited about learning this original language.

The angels told Dee the story of the fallen or wicked angels and how they came to earth and gave humans evil, or black, magic. The angels related to Dee and Kelley that this type of magic should never be used by them. They concluded by telling Dee that he would be the messenger or revealer of the lost knowledge of Enoch. In a sense, he would be the second Enoch. The following are some excerpts of the angelic communications regarding Enoch and Dee's role:

... The Lord appeared unto Enoch, and was mercifull unto him, opened his eyes, that he might see and judge the earth, which was unknown unto his Parents, by reason of their fall: for the Lord said, Let's shew unto Enoch, the use of the earth: And lo, Enoch was wise, and full of the spirit of wisdom. ...

And after 50 dayes Enoch had written: and this was the Title of his books, let those that fear God, and are worthy read.

But behold, the people waxed wicked, and became unrighteous, and the Spirit of the Lord was far off, and gone away from them. So that those that were unworthy began to read. And the Kings of the earth said thus against the Lord, What is it that we cannot do? Or who is he, that can resist us? And the Lord was vexed, and he sent in amongst them an hundred and fifty Lions, and spirits of wickednesse, errour, and deceit: and they appeared unto them: For the Lord had put them between those that are wicked, and his good angels: And they began to counterfeit the doings of God and his power, for they had power given them so to do, so that the memory of Enoch washed away: and the spirits of errour began to teach them Doctrines: which from time to time unto this age, and unto this day, hath spread abroad into all parts of the world, and is the skill and cunning of the wicked.

Hereby they speak with the Devils: not because they have power over the Devils, but because they are joyned unto them in the league and Discipline of their own Doctrine.

For behold, as the knowledge of the mystical figures, and the use of their presence is the gift of God delivered to Enoch, and by Enoch his request to the faithfull, that thereby they might have the true use of God's creatures, and of the earth whereon they dwell: So hath the Devil delivered unto the wicked the signs, and tokens of his error and hatred toward God: whereby they in using them, might consent with their fall: and so become partakers with them of their reward, which is eternal damnation.

These they call Characters: a lamentable thing. For by these, many Souls have perished.

Now hath it pleased God to deliver this Doctrine again out of dark-nesse: and to fulfill his promise with thee, for the books of Enoch: To whom he sayeth as he said unto Enoch.

Let those that are worthy understand this, by thee, that it may be one witnesse of my promise toward thee.

Come therefore, O thou Cloud, and wretched darkness, Come forth I say out of this Table: for the Lord again hath opened the earth: and she shall become known to the worthy.[1]

It's clear that the angels intended Dee to be the new Enoch and the revealer of this wisdom to the world again. I believe this message holds relevance for us today because perhaps it's the method that we need to employ in order to rediscover our true being and our relationship with God. Maybe God's magic will bring us back into the presence of God—it will establish our true relationship with him and the universe.

## Dr. Dee's Method of Spiritual Protection

I would like to reiterate an important point that will be applicable to us when we carry out our own magical technique. Dee began all his angelic communications and sessions with intense prayer and sometimes the reading of several psalms. I want to emphasize this since most modern magic practitioners don't do this, and it's my strong belief, as I've stated elsewhere in this book, that it's an essential part of the process. Here are some quotes from the spiritual diaries of Dr. Dee regarding prayer before and after his rituals:

> After our prayers of the 7 Psalms, and my particular invitation and calling for God his help, and the ministry of his good angels. . . .[2]

The seven psalms are the seven penitential psalms that are recited during Lent. They are Psalm 6, 32, 38, 51, 102, 130, and 143. I strongly recommend the recitation of some psalms, or at least one psalm during your Enochian Meditation; examples are given in the box on pages 95–96.

> We presented our selves, ready for instruction receiving, and presumed not to call my good Minister spiritual, but by humble prayer referred all to God his good pleasure.[3]

In the above statement, Dr. Dee reaffirms his humbleness before God and his reliance on God's will for initiating the angelic sessions.

> Very long I prayed in my Oratory and at my Desk to have answer or resolutions of divers doubts which I had noted. . . ."[4]

> I made long, and often prayers of thanks-giving, calling for grace, mercy, and wisdom: with such particular instructions as I had written down the doubts requiring light, or resolution in them.[5]

> After our divers prayers and contestation of our humility. . . .[6]

These statements by Dee show that he didn't just make short prayers to get them out of the way as many of us do (such as when we say grace before meals). He took prayer seriously and reverently, and he specifically states above that he prayed for a very long time and often. He would also use prayer when wicked or evil angels tried to upset the angelic communications.

> But I held on to pray divers Psalms, and at length against the wicked tempters purposely.[7]

### Recommended Psalms (AV)

Please use whichever version of the Bible you feel most comfortable with. I usually read these parts of the following two psalms. Dee always began his angelic sessions with prayers and a reading of the psalms. He usually selected one or more of the penitential psalms (6, 32, 38, 51, 102, 130, and 143).

### Psalm 51:1–15. Create in Me a Clean Heart, O God

Have mercy upon me, O God, according to thy lovingkindness: according unto the multitude of thy tender mercies blot out my transgressions.

Wash me thoroughly from mine iniquity, and cleanse me from my sin.

For I acknowledge my transgressions: and my sin is ever before me.

Against thee, thee only, have I sinned, and done this evil in thy sight: that thou mightest be justified when thou speakest, and be clear when thou judgest.

Behold, I was shapen in iniquity; and in sin did my mother conceive me.

Behold, thou desirest truth in the inward parts: and in the hidden part thou shalt make me to know wisdom.

Purge me with hyssop, and I shall be clean: wash me, and I shall be whiter than snow.

Make me to hear joy and gladness; that the bones which thou hast
broken may rejoice.

Hide thy face from my sins, and blot out all mine iniquities.

Create in me a clean heart, O God; and renew a right spirit within me.

Cast me not away from thy presence; and take not thy holy spirit
from me.

Restore unto me the joy of thy salvation; and uphold me with thy
free spirit.

Then will I teach transgressors thy ways; and sinners shall be con-
verted unto thee.

Deliver me from bloodguiltiness, O God, thou God of my salvation:
and my tongue shall sing aloud of thy righteousness.

O Lord, open thou my lips; and my mouth shall shew forth thy
praise.

## Psalm 104: 1–9. O Lord My God, You're Very Great

Bless the LORD, O my soul. O LORD my God, thou art very great;
thou art clothed with honour and majesty.

Who coverest thyself with light as with a garment: who stretchest
out the heavens like a curtain:

Who layeth the beams of his chambers in the waters: who maketh
the clouds his chariot: who walketh upon the wings of the wind:

Who maketh his angels spirits; his ministers a flaming fire:

Who laid the foundations of the earth, that it should not be removed
for ever.

Thou coveredst it with the deep as with a garment: the waters stood
above the mountains.

At thy rebuke they fled; at the voice of thy thunder they hasted away.

They go up by the mountains; they go down by the valleys unto the
place which thou hast founded for them.

Thou hast set a bound that they may not pass over; that they turn
not again to cover the earth.

## Conducting an Enochian Ritual

In Dee's early conferences with the angels, they instructed him how to construct certain ritual equipment for their communications and for what he would need:

- a holy table
- a special emblem, called the Sigillum Dei Aemeth, which bore the names of the angels on it)
- seven symbols or talismans, called the Ensigns of Creation, to be placed or drawn on the holy table
- a breastplate with symbols on it that was worn about the neck
- a magic ring with the name PELE on it, which means "he who works wonders"
- four small emblems, which were placed under the legs of the holy table to insulate it from the ground

While Kelley peered into the crystal ball to see and hear what the angels were saying, Dee acted like a scribe, recording all that Kelley observed.

## Other Occult Societies and the Enochian Calls

If we move ahead in time, we discover that some of the most well-known magical societies incorporated the Enochian Calls into their magical systems. The founders of the Golden Dawn in the late nineteenth century, S. L. Macgregor Mathers and Wynn Westcott, tried to create or generate a practical way to use Dee's magic in a systematic way. They synthesized a unique approach and, for the most part, they were successful. The only problem was that some of the information they used was inaccurate and their rituals were saturated with procedures made up by them; these rituals had never been part of Dee's angelic communications. That's why I believe we need to go back to Dee's original

Figure 6.1. This is a copy of a scan from one of the pages of the Dee diaries, held by author John DeSalvo. The original diary is in the British Library; this copy is used with their permission.

source material, his diaries, and minimize the amount of material that was added later.

One of the most famous practitioners of angelic or Enochian Magic was Aleister Crowley. He also synthesized a working system based on Dee's information. What he produced was very interesting and coherent, but again, much of the procedures and rituals were of his own invention. He is also known to have entered and explored all thirty Aethyrs. (I will discuss his experiences in a later chapter.)

Today, everyone talks about angels and being able to communicate with them. You can call a 900 number and get information from someone who talks to angels, and there are books too numerous to mention that explore angelic communications. I'm not saying this is bad because this accessibility increases our awareness of the spiritual world and the world of the angels. However, most of these tools and rituals are created by the respective author or practitioner. The reason I wrote *this* book was to present a magical system, or should I say an angelic or Enochian magical system—which is based solely on what Dr. Dee was given by the angels over four hundred years ago—with very little embellishment. (In fact, I point out the embellishments, so feel free to eliminate them.)

The Enochian Calls, as we will see, are much different than the grimoires of medieval times. The magical grimoires were based on a work called the Keys of Solomon, which allegedly was a manual of how King Solomon invoked and controlled angels and demons. These grimoires (basically a textbook of magic), used the divine names of God and the names of angels to control and command angels to do the magician's bidding.

Dee's Enochian Magic is quite different. For example, there are no Hebrew names of God in the Angelic Calls themselves and no specific names of the angels such as Gabriel, Raphael, and others. Instead the Calls only have descriptive names of the angels (powerful, majestic, etc.). Also, the Calls are more like statements and properties of God and the angels, rather than requests or demands. When using the grimoires, the magician usually decided when to initiate or terminate a session. Not so with the Dee angelic communications. The angels themselves decided when to start or end a session.

## A Scientific Theory of How It Works

Finally, I would like to address what I believe is the scientific basis of Enochian Magic. Enochian Magic works, but not as a result of the imagination working overtime or the wishful thinking or subconscious activity of the magician. Enochian Magic is real, and the Aethyrs and angels are real worlds and real beings.

My theory as to why and how it works is the following: I believe that our brains—most likely our cortical areas, which are responsible for our higher brain functioning and the interpretation of our sensory input (sight, sound, touch, taste, and smell)—are also responsible for receiving psychic information. Although it's believed that we use less than 10 percent of our entire brain, no one knows for sure exactly what this percentage is. Perhaps some part of this unused part of our brain is used for psychic transmission and reception.

I believe there are undiscovered cortical regions, which code for and are receptors of psychic phenomena, in the same way that our retinas enable us to see by functioning as receptors of light rays. We're capable of entering each Aethyr when that brain area becomes activated as a result of reciting a Call. In so doing, we also become aware of the angels residing in that region. The pineal gland, which is a structure in the direct center of our brain that many cultures claim is a psychic center, may also house psychic reception centers.

In Eastern meditation, a verbal mantra is employed as part of the practice. It's a resonating sound, which causes changes in the nervous system. That's why the meditating individual relaxes and enters a deep trance and an altered state of consciousness. The same is true of the Enochian Calls. They are like long mantras, which stimulate specific areas of the brain responsible for the awareness of each of the thirty Aethyrs and their angels.

I hope that this theory can be eventually tested by measuring activity in the magician's cortical areas while he or she is experiencing an Enochian Meditation and entering the Aethyrs. Such a clinical study would indeed show whether or not specific regions of the brain are activated with each Call. If these areas can be identified and mapped, we certainly would have some interesting neurophysiological verification of Enochian Magic and how it works! This exciting neurophysiologic research could also produce incredible breakthroughs in research involving altered states of consciousness.

Until we can demonstrate that Enochian Magic has a scientific basis, we're only left with what we can experience. I believe the specific technique that I'll be teaching you has the greatest potential for you to be successful in opening up these dormant centers in your brain and allowing you to explore these Heavens or Aethyrs for yourself.

# 1

# THE TRANSMISSION
# OF THE ENOCHIAN
# TABLES AND THE
# FORTY-EIGHT CALLS

What exactly are the forty-eight Enochian Calls or Keys, how do we use them, and how were they transmitted to Dee and Kelley by the angels? We must keep in mind there were two types of information transmitted to Dee and Kelly. The first was a set of so-called tables that contained grids of letters and numbers (that were sometimes used to generate the Calls): the second were the Calls themselves.

The angels said that the tables comprised the most important book ever given to humans; it has been called the "Book of the Speech of God." This book, they were told, would restore the knowledge that God originally gave humans. The angels also imply that the restoration of this information may have something to do with the end times, and this restoration of information may be responsible for bringing in a new era or age to our planet. Here are some extracts of the angel's words regarding these tables, which I've modernized where appropriate:

> In those Tables are contained the mystical and holy voices of the angels: dignified . . . which pierceth Heaven, and looketh into the Center of the Earth: the very language and speech of Children and

Innocents, such as magnify the name of God, and are pure. . . . These Tables are to be written, not by man, but by the finger of her which is mother to Virtue. . . . These things and mysteries are your parts, and portions sealed, as well by your own knowledge, as the fruit of your Intercession.[1]

Oute of this, shall be restored the holy bokes, which have perished euen from the begynning, and from the first that Liued. And herin shall be deciphered perfect truths from imperfect falsehode, True religion from fals and damnable errors, . . . which we prepre to the vse of man, the first and sanctified perfection: Which when it hath spread a While, THEN COMMETH THE ENDE.[2]

These tables were quite large. In fact, each table was composed of forty-nine rows and forty-nine columns. This yielded 2,401 empty squares or cells (49 × 49 = 2,401). Each of these cells was filled in with a letter or a number or was left blank. The angels communicated to Kelley the exact letter or number to place in each of these empty cells or squares. These were communicated by the angels in Latin, not Enochian, and were written into the chart by Kelley in Latin (which is the same as the Roman alphabet we use today). This is a deviation from the established routine because just about all the diaries and other angelic communications involving Dee and Kelley appear to have been written in the hand of Dr. Dee. (I believe that Dee had his own handwritten copies of the tables; please see the epilogue for further discussion of this point.)

The final product was ninety-five tables* (each containing 2,401

---

*Something very interesting happened to me in the course of my research, with regard to the tables. There are ninety-five original tables in the British Library, but what does not jive is that the angels refer to these tables as the set of "forty-nine tables," and in actual fact, we only access forty-eight tables. How do we go from ninety-five to forty-nine to forty-eight? Of course, I had to look into the matter. It took a little legwork and some more analytical thinking, but I resolved the conundrum and felt like Sherlock Holmes in so doing. It was a very exciting moment for me, but because it's a discussion that is not entirely germane to our general discourse—but *does* make for interesting reading—I have included it as appendix A in the back of the book for those who are as curious as I was about this matter.

cells filled with letters or numbers). Multiplying 95 by 2,401 gives 228,095 spaces. Thus, the angels had to specify over two hundred thousand letters or numbers to fill each of the empty cells. (Actually it was less than that since in some of the tables, only every other cell was filled in. In general, however, we're talking about a large number of letters and numbers to be transmitted from the angelic world to our world.)

The other issue was that the angels told Dee and Kelley that they had to complete these tables in forty days, which they actually did. The task commenced on March 29, 1583, and culminated on May 6, 1583, exactly thirty-nine days after they had first begun.

The angels also instructed Dee and Kelley to eventually rewrite the tables, replacing the Latin letters with the Enochian equivalent of those letters. (The angels had given Kelley and Dee a translation key between the Enochian and Latin; please see figure 7.1 on page 112.) It appears, however, the Kelley and Dee never undertook to translate the Latin to Enochian, or if they did, the location of these tables (if they still exist) is unknown.

How did the angels convey to Dee and Kelley the letters that fill in the grids of the tables? At first, it appears that an angel pointed to a letter (found on the set of tables in the Book of Enoch that the angel held) with a rod, and at the same time, the angel also pronounced the letter. Kelley "saw" the letter and also "heard" the pronunciation and then wrote it down. It's interesting to note that Leonardo da Vinci said that angels can't speak or make sounds since air must be moved in order to do this. In accordance with this, it seems likely that Kelley saw and heard the Calls psychically and not through physical emanations.

Later, in order to speed up the process, the angels didn't pronounce the letters but only pointed to them with the rod, at which point Kelley would say them out loud. It's interesting that Kelley couldn't read the letters until some supernatural fire or energy flashed into his head and he went into some kind of trance. This happened many times during the transmission of the tables. When the energy left his head, he came out of the trance. In Dee's diary is a description of this:

A voyce: Read.

[Edward Kelly] EK: I cannot.

Dee: Then there flashed fire upon EK agayne.

A voyce: Say what thow thinkest.

EK: My hed is all on fire.

A voyce: What thow thinkest, euery word, that speak.

EK: I can read all, now, most perfectly.

Kelley went on to read the letters that the angel pointed to and, at the end of the session, came out of the trance state.

Dee: The fire cam from EK his eyes, and went into the stone againe. And then, he couldn't perceyue, or red one worde.[3]

## The Generation of the Calls from the Tables

After the tables were assembled, the next step would be to generate the forty-eight Enochian Calls from them. How was this done, exactly? We have more specifics about this since Dee recorded more details about this procedure in his diary. The angel who appeared in Kelley's crystal had his set of tables and would point to a specific grid location on one of the tables. Kelley would observe that letter or number and the location and give this information to Dee, but not simply by its row and column but by some cryptic numbers and descriptions. No one has been able to figure out what these cryptic numbers and descriptions mean. Dee, using these descriptions, would find the correlating position on his copy of the tables and then write that number or letter down.

What did these numbers and descriptions refer to? Let's look at some of these strange directions, with numbers too large to indicate grid coordinates, which Kelley gave to Dee. Here is an example of the exact words the angels used in specifying a grid location:

The exact Center excepted.

A (Two thousand and fourteen, in the sixth Table, is) D

86. 7003. In the thirteenth Table is I.

A In the 21th. Table. 11405 downward.

I In the last Table, one lesse then Number. A word, Jaida you shall understand, what that word is before the Sun go down. Jaida is the last word of the call.

85. H 49. ascending T 49. descending, A 909. directly, O simply.

H 2029. directly, call it Hoath.[4]

Dee was a cartographer and cryptologist, and when he returned to England, he brought with him two great globes manufactured by Mercator. Perhaps the large numbers and strange descriptions were geographic coordinates (latitude and longitude). Perhaps some other cryptic method was used, relating to some other kind of coordinates. No one has been able to figure this out yet.

In any event, after the angels located the letters or numbers for Kelley and Dee using this strange method, they abandoned it to use a simpler procedure, in which they gave Dee and Kelley the letters or numbers directly, pointing to them on the table or on one of the aforementioned globes that had letters on them. It is interesting that the angels only used this method with the strange coordinates for the first nineteen words of the First Call only. They obviously didn't think it was necessary to continue with this tedious and confusing method. They then used the following method, as explained by Kelly:

He hath a rod or wand in his hand, almost as big as my little finger: it's of Gold, and divided into three equal parts, with a brighter Gold than the rest. He standeth upon his round table of Christal, or rather Mother of Pearl: There appear an infinite number of letters on the same, as thick as one can stand by another. The table is somewhat inclined on one side: he standeth in the very middle. . . .[5]

He smit the round Table with his rod; and it whirled about with a great swiftness. Now that which before seemed to be a circular and plain form, appeareth to be a Globe and round Ball; corporal, when it turneth. . . . He striketh the Table now, and though the body seem to turn, yet the Letter seem to stand still in their places. . . . Read backward. . . .[6]

The angels also gave Kelley an English version of all the Calls by the following method:

And now Nalvage [the angel] is on the top of the Globe, and his seat remaineth in the former manner of fire. Now Nalvage holdeth up his right hand, and the same seemeth to be many hands. There is on one of his fingers an I. It vanisheth away; and so on divers fingers are words as follow. I Reign over you saith the God of Justice. . . .[7]

For another Call, Kelley describes again how the English version is given:

Now he holdeth up many hands and fingers as before, and on the very end of the fingers distinctly these parcels [of words] appeared in English.[8]

Also, and as mentioned previously, the angels initially spelled out the Calls in reverse order because, according to them, the Calls were so powerful that they didn't want to cause any supernatural event to upset the transmission process:

Nalvage: Also in receiving of the calls, this is to be noted: that they are to be uttered of me, backward: and of you, in practice, forward.

Dee: I understand it, for the efficacity of them; else, all things called would appear: and so hinder our proceeding in learning.[9]

Beginning at the fifth key to the last one, they abandoned the reverse order procedure and, in order to speed up the process, gave Kelley and Dee the Calls in the direct letter sequence in which they were to be read.

As we know, Dee noted the pronunciations of the Calls in the margins of his diaries. But where did Dee get the information about *how* the Enochian Calls (constructed from the dictated letters) were to be pronounced? Did he just guess or was this specific information revealed to him by the angels?

I think that this information on the proper pronunciations came directly from the angels. I searched throughout the sections on the transmission of the Calls and found a statement that I believe proves this. On page 95 of Casaubon's book, the angel is transmitting the words of one of the Calls to Kelly. At one point, the angel gives Kelly the word *Amiran*. Then the angel tells Dee to "sound your word." Dee then says, "Amiran."

It appears that the angel then pronounces the word to Kelly to indicate the *proper* pronunciation. Kelly says. "He pronounceth the I so remissely, as it is scare heard, and in the pronouncing of the whole word he seemeth not to move his lips." Whether all the Enochian words were verified like this remains unknown. It is possible the ones that Dee did not pronounce properly, as in the example above, were corrected right away by the angel.

I've used all of the information from the diaries and the marginal notations to put together what I believe is the most accurate pronunciation of the Calls used to open the thirty Aethyrs or Heavens. (Please refer to the accompanying CD for these pronunciations.) The angels Gabriel, Mapsama, and Nalvage made some very powerful comments about these forty-eight Calls. One of the most powerful angelic statements in all of the Dee diaries was that these keys are treasures worth more than the frames of the heavens:

Gabriel: Thus hath God kept promise with you, and hath delivered you the keys of his storehouses: wherein you shall find (if you enter wisely, humbly, and patiently) Treasures more worth than the frames of the heavens.[10]

We have other statements from other angels about the Calls:

Mapsama: God hath opened unto you, his Judgment: He hath delivered unto you the keyes that you may enter; But be humble. Enter not of presumption, but of permission. Go not in rashly; But be brought in willingly: For many have ascended, but few have entred.[11]

Nalvage: It's the sense in your tongue of the holy and mystical Call before delivered: . . . Wherein, they will open the mysteries of their creation, as far as shall be necessary: and give you understanding of many thousand secrets, wherein you're yet but children; for every Table hath his key: every key openeth his gate, and every gate being opened, gives knowledge of himself of entrance, and of the mysteries of those things whereof he is an inclosure. Within these Palaces you shall find things that are of power. . . .[12]

The angel Nalvage also said:

Unto this Doctrine belongeth the perfect knowledge and remembrance of the mysticall Creatures.[13]

The transmission of the forty-eight Calls from the tables began in April of 1584 and was completed around July of that same year.

In reality, there are forty-nine Calls, but only forty-eight Calls were given to Dee and Kelley. The First Call was never given since the angels said that it was to be only of God; it was too powerful and sublime for humans to know or comprehend. The angel Nalvage explains why the First Call was not given to them:

I finde the Soul of man hath no portion in this first Table. It's the Image of the son of God, in the bosom of his father, before all the worlds. It comprehends his incarnation, passion, and return to judgment: which he himself, in flesh, knoweth not; all the rest are of understanding.[14]

# The Nineteenth Call

We will only be using the last thirty of the forty-eight Calls in our meditation. The angels transmitted eighteen Calls to Kelley and Dee, and when they came to the nineteenth, they made it clear that this Nineteenth Call was to be used only to generate the thirty additional Calls. They also made it clear that the thirty additional Calls were the ones to be used to enter the thirty Aethyrs.

Thus, many occultists divide Enochian Magic into two branches: the elemental that uses the first eighteen Calls and the aethyrical that uses the thirty Calls of the Aethyrs.

Here is a translation of the Nineteenth Call:

### English Translation of the Nineteenth Call
### (Thirty Calls of the Aethyrs)

O you heavens which dwell in the First [or Second, Third, Fourth, or whichever Aethyr you are exploring] Air are mighty in the parts of the earth and execute the judgments of the highest to you. It's said, behold the face of your God, the beginning of comfort whose eyes are the brightness of the heavens, which provided you for the government of the earth, and her unspeakable variety, furnishing you with a power, understanding to dispose all things according to the providence of him that sitteth on the holy Throne, and rose up in the beginning saying, the earth, let her be governed by her parts; and let there be division in her, that the glory of her may be always drunken and vexed in itself. Her course, let it run with the Heavens, and as a handmaid. Let her serve them one season: Let it confound another, and let there be no creature upon, or within her the same. All her members let them differ in their qualities, and let there be no one creature equal with another. The reasonable creatures of the earth, or Man. Let them vex and weed out one another, and the dwelling places, let them forget their names, the work of man and his pomp: Let them be defaced his buildings, let them become caves for the beasts of the field, confound her understanding with darkness, for why? It repenteth me I made man one while let her be known, and another while a stranger, because she is the bed of a harlot and the dwelling place of Him that is fallen. O you havens arise, the lower heavens underneath you, let them serve you. Govern those that govern, cast down such as fall, bring forth with those that increase, and destroy the rotten. No place, let it remain in one number. Add and diminish until the stars be numbered; arise, Move, and appear before the Covenant of his mouth, which he hath sworn unto us in his Justice. Open the mysteries of your Creation, and make us partakers of undefiled knowledge.

## The Enochian Alphabet

Now, let's look briefly at the Enochian alphabet, which consists of twenty-one characters. The angels tried to guide Kelley in drawing this Enochian alphabet but were not successful. Therefore, they did the following. The angels caused the Enochian characters to appear on Kelley's paper in a light yellow color. Kelley would then take his pen and trace the letters. Once done, the yellow glow would disappear, and Kelley was left with his ink tracing.

One of the reasons (there are possibly more) that the angels gave Kelley and Dee this alphabet was so that they could translate the letters

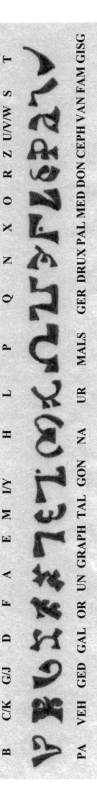

Figure 7.1. The twenty-one characters of the Enochian alphabet. This alphabet, which Kelley traced, appears on the last page of the Book of Enoch (i.e., the tables). I've redrawn these letters with our alphabet on top and the name of each letter underneath.

and numbers in the tables into Enochian, as they instructed. However, and as we know, this apparently was never done. Language experts, who have studied the Enochian words, concluded that the Enochian language has a grammar and syntax all its own.

One character (that looks like a *Z*) represents a different English letter by putting a dot next to it. Also, four of the letters represent more than one English letter. Thus, we have equivalents for all twenty-six letters of the English alphabet. Anything written in these characters can be translated into the English alphabet. Enochian is read from right to left like Hebrew. For example, the Enochian word shown in plate 11 of the color insert can be translated into English as BAPPOMGEL. (If you want to have some fun, try constructing your name with the Enochian alphabet!)

Now let's get back to the Calls. As we now know, eighteen Calls were initially given to Kelley and Dee. It was then made clear to them that the Nineteenth Call would be unique in that it was only to be used to generate thirty additional Calls. It was these thirty additional Calls that would be used to enter each of the thirty Aethyrs or heavenly realms. Thus, the first eighteen Calls plus the thirty Calls generated from the nineteenth would total forty-eight individual Calls (18 + 30 = 48).

## The Generation of the Thirty Calls

How the thirty Calls were generated from the Nineteenth Call is very simple. One word, at the third place in the Nineteenth Call, was changed thirty times. This third word was the specific name of one of the thirty Aethyrs or Heavens that the Call would open up. Thus, each of the thirty Calls of the Aethyrs are identical except for one word.

Let me give an example. The first two words of the Nineteenth Call are "Madriax dspraf." The third word is the specific name of one of the thirty Aethyrs. The name of the First Aethyr is "LIL," the Second is "ARN," and so on. So if you were going to generate the Call for the First

Aethyr, you would say: "Madriax dspraf LIL . . ." and continue with the rest of the Call. To generate the Second Call, you would substitute the name of the Second Aethyr, which is ARN, in the third place; thus, "Madriax dspraf ARN . . ." The rest of the thirty Calls are generated the same way—by substituting the name of the specific Aethyr in the third place of the Nineteenth Call.

As we know, each Aethyr is ruled or governed by specific angels called governors. The angels had given Dee and Kelly the names of the ninety-one governors of the Aethyrs about two months earlier on May 21, 1584, by pointing to the letters on the table or on the globe:

EK: Now he standeth on the top of the Table.[15]

I assume that the angel is either pointing to the letters on the table or on the globe as he usually does.

Each Aethyr has three governors except for the thirtieth, which has four. Thus, we have a total of ninety-one angels, or governors, ruling the thirty Aethyrs ($4 + [29 \times 3] = 91$). These angels or governors are sometimes called princes. The angels have said that each Aethyr is divided into three areas or parts, and each of the three parts is ruled by one of the three governors of that Aethyr (except for the Thirtieth Aethyr, which is divided into four parts and has four governors). The angels also point out that each of the ninety-one areas comprising the thirty Aethyrs corresponds to or has a relationship with a specific location on earth.

The angels gave more specifics regarding these governors. The ninety-one governors are spirits of the air element. Also, their powers are not all equal, and their mansions or realms are not all alike. They are ruled by the twelve tribes of Israel, who are, in turn, ruled by the seven angelic beings before the throne of God. This is explained by the angel Nalvage:

Those 30 are the Calls of . . . Princes and spiritual Governours, unto whom the Earth is delivered as a portion. These bring in and again . . . Kings and all the Governments upon the Earth, and vary the

Natures of things: with the variation of every moment; Unto whom the providence of the eternal Judgment is already opened. These are generally governed by the twelve Angels of the 12 Tribes: which are also governed by the 7 which stand before the presence of God. Let him that can see look up; and let him that can hear [sic], attend; for this is wisdom. They are all spirits of the Air: not rejected, but dignified; and they dwell and have their habitation in the air diversely, and in sundry places: for their mansions are not alike, neither are their powers equal. Understand therefore, that from the fire to the earth, there are 30 places or abidings: one above and beneath another: wherein these aforesaid Creatures have their abode, for a time.[16]

Books on Enochian Magic contain the specific name of each Aethyr, the governors of those Aethyrs, the regions on earth associated with each governor, the tribe ruling each governor, and the angel of the presence ruling those angels of the tribes. Some tables also give the number of ministers under each angel of the tribe, the compass direction where each angel of the tribe resides, and the name of the angelic kings ruling the twelve tribes. We will not be concerned with most of this information but only the names of the governors and the specific Aethyrs that they rule. (If you're interested, Lon Milo DuQuette's book, *Enochian Vision Magick,* contains all of this information.)

Now that Dee had the forty-eight Angelic Calls, which included the thirty Calls of the Aethyrs, what did he do with them? There is no indication that he actually practiced angelic magic and used the Calls to enter the Aethyrs and communicate with the governors of each Aethyr. There are some statements by the angels that seem to imply he was not supposed to use any of this until they gave him permission or the time was right. Some scholars believe this knowledge was meant for a future time or generation. Others believe he did practice it and either didn't record it in his diaries, or these diaries were lost or destroyed. I personally believe Dee practiced this type of magic, especially later in his life, and that he did explore the Aethyrs and communicated with the governors.

I find it interesting that the angels in the above quote say that their powers are not equal and their mansions are not alike. This is important in our meditation since we will discover that each governor has a unique presence, which I call a flavor. Also, the mansions have different locations within each Aethyr. It's known by magicians and occultists that there are spirits of the different elements: fire, air, water, and earth. For some reason, all of the ninety-one governors of the thirty Aethyrs are comprised of the element of air.

As we know, the angels further explained to Dee that the thirty Aethyrs or spiritual worlds surround our physical realm. Each one penetrates higher and higher into the spiritual realms toward God. It's the goal of humans to traverse these Aethyrs, starting with the lowest and moving to the highest. The angels called the lowest, most physical Aethyr (the closest one to the earth) number thirty. As one moves higher into the spiritual dimension, one approaches "one," which is the highest spiritual Aethyr one can enter, and this is the closest one to God.

A word should be said about the first eighteen Calls, which we won't be using. We really don't know for sure what they activate or who they invoke, but since the time of Dee, many magical groups and practitioners have formed their own theories about this. It does seem that these eighteen Calls are associated with accessing the unseen elemental world (the unseen spirits associated with the elements of fire, air, earth, and water) and are used to contact the angels and spirits residing there.

If you would like to learn more about this, I would again refer you to Lon Milo DuQuette's book.

Let's now move on to the actual practice of the Enochian Meditation.

# 8

# HOW TO PRACTICE THE ENOCHIAN MEDITATION— A PRACTICAL GUIDE

This chapter will be your instruction manual on how to carry out your own personal Enochian ritual or, as I prefer to call it, the Enochian Meditation. You will learn its proper preparation, how to perform it, and the procedure to properly end it. You may want to read the entire book before you begin this meditation so that you will understand all of the variables involved. On the other hand, you may be more open and not want to be influenced by reading the experiences of others before you try it for yourself. You decide.

## Specifics on the Enochian Meditation

Why do I use the term *meditation* instead of *ritual*? I personally don't like the word *ritual* since it conjures up individuals in black robes using lots of elaborate equipment. I don't believe my technique fits into this category—it's essentially a magical meditation. Thus, I believe it's best described as the Enochian Meditation since, after all, it's a meditation using Enochian Magic. I will continue to refer to it as Enochian Meditation, or EM for short.

In my thirty years of spiritual searching and after having read hundreds of how-to books on meditation, psychic development, contacting your guardian angel, astral projection, psychometry, magical path working, and scrying (to name just a few subjects), I've never found any psychic or magical technique that really worked for me, except for the technique described in Lon Milo DuQuette's book, *Enochian Vision Magick*. I think the basic problem is that many of the techniques in the how-to books are just too complicated, take too long to learn or develop, and require props and apparatuses. I've tried many of the Golden Dawn and OTO rituals on my own and have bought books on popular or do-it-yourself magic and tried their techniques as well. I've also received personal guidance by several experienced magicians. All in all, except for a few isolated instances, I didn't achieve any significant or notable results with any of these methods.

Most people want something that's easy to do and effective right away. That's why I developed the Enochian Meditation technique. It uses no ritual equipment or props, except this book and a candle (which is optional). You should be able to accomplish the process in about thirty to forty minutes and, hopefully, get results the first time you do it. I had results my first time and continue to get results almost every time I do the technique.

I know that not everyone may experience the same outcome. No technique will be 100 percent successful for every reader, but I do believe my technique has a higher probability of working than any other magical technique available. I also believe that simplicity is the key to any successful technique, and given this, I don't think I could have developed a simpler or more efficient process.

Simplicity seems to be a universal theme in the field of science. Physicists believe that, if a unified field equation is ever developed (an equation that mathematically describes all the forces in nature, large and small, such as gravity and quantum mechanics), it will be a short and simple one. Most of the greatest equations in physics and mathematics are simple and elegant. I'm thinking specifically of Einstein's General and Special Theory of Relativity, Newton's equations, and Maxwell's equations, to name just a few. Get a good general physics book, look these up, and you will see what I mean.

The greatest equation with the greatest simplicity is the Pythagorean Theorem. As you may recall from high school math, this theorem dictates that the square of the length of the hypotenuse of a right triangle equals the sum of the squares of the lengths of the other two sides. Pythagoras was also a mystic, and it's no wonder that he's credited with the discovery of this simple and most important relationship in geometry. Lon Milo DuQuette, an authority on Enochian Magic who wrote the foreword to this book, told me that even if you have almost no ability for magic, you can get results with Enochian Magic; it's that powerful![1] That was good news for me since I've always felt that I fit in the "no ability for magic" category. He also told me that in his many years of using Enochian Magic, he had never experienced any negative side effects from practicing it.

I've been doing Transcendental Meditation for more than thirty years, and the first time I performed the Enochian Meditation, I experienced a more profound and deeper trance then I ever had experienced while doing TM. I was once monitored with physiological equipment during my TM meditation, and the equipment documented a drop in my heart rate, body temperature, lowering of brain wave amplitude, and other physiological effects consistent with deep rest and a lowering of the body's metabolism. It has also been shown that TM produces an increase in alpha brain wave activity, signifying deep rest and relaxation. This is a unique state and doesn't usually happen in sleep, hypnosis, a coma, or any other known state of consciousness.

In fact, I feel I go into a much deeper state, more quickly, with the Enochian Meditation. I've not had my physiological variables measured during a Enochian Meditation, but I hope to be able to test this in the near future. I continue to use both Enochian Meditation and Transcendental Meditation; each one has a different value for me.

The Enochian Meditation also seems to give one an unusual

amount of energy. You may go into the meditation a little tired or fatigued and come out of it refreshed and full of energy. This makes sense because you're touching the source of your being, which is God. It renews you and energizes the physical, mental, and spiritual bodies of which you're comprised. It makes sense that, if you're contacting your deepest spiritual being, it will reflect in other realities, in the mental and physical worlds. Remember the saying "as above, so below"? I like to rephrase it like this: "as in our inner spirit body or innermost being where God dwells, so in our physical and mental bodies."

Anyone with psychological problems should not attempt to perform magic. Too many people have gotten into trouble this way. They should first resolve their issues with the help of a licensed psychologist or psychiatrist. You must have a stable mind and, in a sense, a normal psyche to do magic. In fact, Israel Regardie, one of the most famous of the Golden Dawn magicians, felt that someone should undergo a long period of counseling before they even begin the practice of magic.

I've mentioned that some of the most common experiences of God's Meditation are the feelings of peace, calm, and balance. I think balance is the key to spiritual enlightenment. When we're balanced—physically, mentally, and spiritually—we escape the bounds of time and creation and exist in the timeless presence of God. The Eastern religions call this liberation or the attainment of nirvana. The Buddha called it "The Nothingness." In Zen, it's referred to as absolute stillness. Some in the West call it cosmic consciousness. Other religions have different names for this experience.

It's really a balance between positive and negative. Visualize a seesaw with positive on one side and negative on the other. The goal is to be in the center, at the fulcrum, detached and free from the bonds of space and time. I believe God is at the center of this fulcrum, and when we're perfectly balanced, we're one with him and have reached our spiritual goal. Through the ages, many techniques have been developed to achieve this balance; these include meditation, contemplation, prayer, yoga, Zen, and numerous other religious, mystical, and occult practices. (Please see plates 12 and 13 of the color insert for illustrations of balancing tools.)

I believe magic is one of the best and most natural God-given means to accomplish this balance, and that's why I wrote this book. The meditation contained herein attempts to recreate this balance for its participants. As we go through the thirty Aethyrs, perhaps each one will balance a certain aspect of our spiritual nature. Could it be that the goal is to center ourselves in all these Aethyrs and balance all of them simultaneously? As each Aethyr becomes balanced, we move closer to the point where only God is present.

I need to reiterate a primary theme expressed throughout this book. The purpose of magic—and, in my opinion, its only purpose— is to experience God and his good angels, to become close to him, and to experience his love, presence, and light. Magic is a spiritual technique to put us in touch with God, who resides in our innermost being. As such, it's a gift from him to help us on our spiritual path and journey toward him. We don't have to travel anywhere to find him. We just need to go deep within ourselves to make contact with him.

I want to point out that the Enochian Meditation parallels many of the procedures of a church service. There are opening and closing prayers, readings, and meditations. There are other very interesting parallels that you will experience for yourself. I guess in a way this meditation is my form of going to church, but it was only after many months of practicing it that I realized the similarities. The big difference is that to me, this is my *real* church, since I'm coming in contact with God directly and experiencing his being for myself.

In the Enochian Meditation, there are thirty Aethyrs we can explore, one by one, by conducting separate sessions for each one. The usual procedure is to start at the Thirtieth Aethyr (the lowest or closest to the earth and farthest from God) and work your way up to the

First (the highest one spiritually or the one that's closest to God). We may not be able to enter all of them, and how far we get may depend on our level of spiritual development and awareness, which is as it should be.

After further spiritual development, perhaps we can go further and continue on our path. We're all different and are at different places in our spiritual ascent toward God. Don't rush anything. Also, please refer to the CD that accompanies this book for specifics on different parts of the meditative procedure, including the correct pronunciations of the entire Enochian Call.

Even though I believe the following meditation is safe and helpful, I want to state that the author and the publishers of this book are not responsible for the effects or results of this technique. I suggest that you be sure to follow the correct procedures. Also, please know that this meditation isn't necessarily for everyone; you have to decide whether or not it's right for you. The minimum criteria are that:

- You don't have any physical or mental problems that could interfere or cause any problems for you.
- Your purpose in doing this is to become closer to God and to experience his peace, knowledge, and wisdom—and not for any selfish, material reason.
- You follow the specifics of the procedure and learn them well before you attempt to modify it to your own individual needs.

The entire meditation should take thirty to forty minutes if it's not rushed. It should be done with devotion and love. I like to think that I'm on holy ground when I do it.

## The Lesser Banishing Ritual of the Pentagram

You will perform the Lesser Banishing Ritual of the Pentagram both before and after the Enochian Meditation. As stated earlier, employing the LBRP is a way to purify your environment and protect yourself from any negative energies or entities.

The LBRP only takes a few minutes to do. It's extremely important that, as with any magical procedure, you treat the LBRP with respect and reverence. You're dealing with forces that we know little about. Just because your motives may be pure doesn't necessarily protect you from its consequences. I will give you an example using electricity as an analogy. To use, experiment with, or tap the energy of electricity, you have to know how to handle it properly and safely. You may have good intentions, but if you put your finger in a wall outlet, you will be electrocuted. In a similar fashion, just because you have good intentions with regard to magic doesn't mean you'll be safe. This is a misconception that many people have.

The LBRP is so ancient that no one really knows where it originated; it has lasted through eons of time because it's so effective. Almost every time I do the LBRP, I feel extreme peace and quiet, and the atmosphere around me seems pure.

An interesting effect is that after you perform the LBRP, your mind seems to quiet down too; there isn't a constant chatter of thoughts going on. After performing it, I always feel as if I've taken a bath in the light, love, and purity of God. I feel the peace of the universe, the oneness.

## The Enochian Meditation–Step-by-Step

The meditation is divided into three parts as follows.

### Part One—Preparation and Preliminaries

This consists of the initial setup of the area you will be meditating in, the conducting of the preliminary visualizations and prayers, and an enactment of the Lesser Banishing Ritual of the Pentagram, which is comprised of the Kabbalistic Cross and the Pentagram of White Light. This normally takes five to ten minutes.

*Part Two—The Enochian Meditation Itself*

This consists of reading aloud the entire Enochian Call and meditating on the governors' names (the angels in charge of the Aethyr you're trying to enter, experience, and explore). Reading the Enochian Call out loud is the main thrust of this meditation. (I suggest you don't meditate longer than fifteen minutes at first. You can increase the time after you feel comfortable with the procedure.)

*Part Three—Ending the Meditation*

This consists of thanking the governors or angels, reading the License to Depart and the final prayer, and performing the Lesser Banishing Ritual of the Pentagram. This usually takes about ten minutes.

# THE ENOCHIAN MEDITATION

## Part One—Preparation and Preliminaries

### Seat Yourself Comfortably in a Chair Near a Lighted Candle

Find a quiet place where you will not be disturbed by anyone or by any phone calls. Sit comfortably in a chair and place a lighted candle near you. (Make sure the candle is in a stable position where you can see the flame clearly at all times and where it will not fall or cause anything near it to catch on fire; never leave a candle unattended.) The candle helps you visualize the Light of God and connects you to that light.

### Take a Few Minutes to Relax and Pray

Look at the candle. Think of God and his presence within you. The light from the candle symbolizes the Light of God and connects you to him. Be natural and approach this effortlessly. Don't force any thoughts or feelings. This is a time to take a few minutes to settle down and realize that you're doing this meditation to be present with God and the angels and to experience higher spiritual realms. Recite the psalms and Dee's prayer or make up your own. If you're a member of another denomination, you may choose to read something from your holy book or your prayer book. Everyone is different and has different spiritual needs, so do whatever feels best for you.

### Perform the White Light Visualization
Say the following to yourself and visualize the light (close your eyes to visualize better):

> May the white light surround me.
> May the white light elevate me and put me in touch with my spiritual guides.
> May the white light connect me with the Divine Light, the Light of God.

### Repeat Dr. Dee's (Modified) Prayer
### (This is optional; if repeated, it should be read silently)
O God, I most humbly beg your Divine Mercy to send me the help of some pious wise man and expert philosopher. And if no such mortal man is now living on earth, then I beg you to send me from Heaven your good spiritual ministers and angels, namely Michael, Gabriel, Raphael, and Uriel, and any other true and faithful angels of yours who may instruct me.

### Do the Lesser Banishing Ritual of the Pentagram
### (Do this standing and read the words out loud)
First you will first do the Kabbalistic Cross, and then you will construct the Pentagram of White Light. (The Kabbalistic Cross is similar to the sign of the cross, but the words and directions are different.)

#### The Kabbalistic Cross
- Stand facing east.
- Visualize the Light of God coming to you and just hovering over your head in a dazzling radiant ball of light.

- Reach up with your right index finger and, touching this ball of light, bring it to your forehead and touch your forehead.
- Say or chant: AH-TEH (Unto Thee . . .).
- Move straight down and touch your chest or stomach and say or chant: MAL-KUTH (. . . the Kingdom . . .). (As you move your finger to each part of your body, visualize the white Light of God moving with you, and at the end, you will have a large cross over your body from the white light.)
- Touch your right shoulder and say or chant: VEE-GE-BUR-AH (. . . and the Power . . .).
- Touch your left shoulder and say or chant: VEE-GE DU-LAH (. . . and the Glory . . .).
- Finally, bring your hands together in front of you like in prayer and say or chant: LE-OL-LAM (. . . Forever . . .). AH-MEN.

(I would suggest chanting as it gives this ritual more life and energy. Also, do not repeat the English translations of the words given above in parentheses. This is just for your information.)

**The Pentagram of White Light**

- Facing east, trace a pentagram in the air. The size doesn't matter, but I usually make it on the large side. I can visualize it as a white, vibrant, dazzling light, or a blue flame (whichever you can see more easily). As illustrated in figure 8.1 below, start at the lower left side of the pentagram and move in the directions indicated in the figure.
- When the pentagram is complete, thrust your right index finger (which you're using as your magic wand) in the center of the pentagram and say or chant: YOD-A-HAY, VAV-A-HAY.
- Turn and face south.
- Make the same pentagram again in the air (starting at the lower left side) and, when completed, thrust your right index finger in the center and say or chant: AH-DO-NAI.

Figure 8.1. Start at the lower left corner and trace the pentagram in the direction indicated until you come back to the starting point.

- Turn to the west (notice you're going around a circle in a clockwise direction), trace the pentagram, and when completed, thrust your right index finger in the center and say or chant: E-HI-YAY.
- Turn to the north, trace the pentagram, and when completed, thrust your right index finger in the center and say: AH-GA-LA.
- Turn to the east, and don't trace a pentagram but just thrust your finger in the center of the pentagram you traced initially, thus completing a closed circle of four pentagrams, each one facing a cardinal direction (east, south, west, and north). Visualize this circle and the pentagrams as a vibrant light surrounding and protecting you. These four incantations are names of God.
- Still facing east, stretch out your arms in the form of a cross and chant the following:

  *Before me: RA-FAY-EL.*

  *Behind me: GA-BRE-EL.*

  *On my right: ME-CHI-ALE.*

  *On my left: UR-REE-ALE.*

  (You're summoning the four archangels of God—Raphael, Gabriel, Michael, and Uriel—for protection.)

- Keep your arms outstretched and continue by saying:
  *Before me flames the pentagram.*
  *Behind me shines the six-rayed star.*
- Repeat the Kabbalistic Cross once more, and you're now done with the LBRP.

After you have completed the LBRP, remain standing and pause for a few minutes. Just soak in the peace and calmness and then sit down.

## Part Two—The Enochian Meditation Itself

*Read the Entire Enochian Call Below Out Loud*
*(Please note that the correct pronunciation of the Enochian Call*
*in its entirety is repeated on the CD accompanying this book.)*

If this is the first time you're doing this meditation and you want to begin in the Thirtieth Aethyr (which I strongly recommend), you will be saying the name of the Thirtieth Aethyr (TEX) after you say "Mā -drî -iax Ds praf" (as I've indicated below)—and then you will continue reciting the entire rest of the Call out loud. Because it acts like a mantra, therefore, it is most effective if you recite it out loud. You can chant it if that makes you feel more in tune with it. The words are broken into syllables, and pronunciation marks are added to indicate long and short vowels. (Note: The straight line above the vowel indicates a long vowel: ā ē ī ō ū; the caret symbol above the vowel indicates a short vowel: â ê î ô û.)

### The Enochian Call (The Call of the Thirty Aethyrs)

Mā -drî -iax Ds praf (Name of Aethyr, i.e., TEX) ch(k)īs Mi-cā-olz Sa-ā-nir Ca- ōs-go, od fī-sis Bal-zi-zras Ia(ya)-ī-da, Non-ca(sa) Go-hū-lim, Mic(Mīk)-ma A-do-ī-an Mad, I-ā-od Bli-ōrb, Sâ-ba-o-o-ā-ô-na ch(k) īs Lu-cīf-ti-as pe-rīp-sol, ds Ab-ra-ās-sa Non-cf(sf) Ne-tā-â-ib Ca-os-gi od Ti-lb Ad-phaht Dām-ploz, To-ō-at Non-cf(sf) Gmi-cāl-zô-ma L-rāsd Tōf-glo Marb yār-ry I-doi-go od Tor-zulp ia(ya)-ō-daf Go-hōl, Ca-ōs-ga Ta-ba-ord Sa-ā-nir od Chris-tê-os Yr-pō-il Ti-ō-bl, Bus-dir ti-lb No-aln pa-id ors-ba od Dod-rm(rum)-ni Zyl-na. El-zāp-tilb Parm-gi pe-rīp-sax, od ta Q(K)urlst Bo-o-a-pi-S. Lnib(Lmb)-m o-v-cho Symp, od Chris-tê-os Ag-tol-torn Mirc Q Ti-ōb-l Lel. Ton pa-ombd Dil-zmo As-pī-an, od Chris-tê-os Ag L tōr-torn pa-rāch A-symp, Cord-ziz Dod-pal od Fi-falz Ls-mnad, od Farg-t Bams O-ma-ō-as. Co-nīs-bra od A-uâ-vox To-nug, Ors-cāt-bl No-âs-mi Tab-gēs Levith-mong, un-chi(ki) Omp-tilb Ors. Bagel. Mo-ō-ô-ah ol cōrd-ziz. L ca-pī-mâ-o lx-o-māx-ip od ca-cō-casb Go-sâ-a. Ba-glen pi-i Ti-ān-ta A-bā-bâ-lond, od fa-ōrgt Te-lōc-vo-vim. Mā-drî-iax Tor-zu O-ād-riax Or-ō-cha(ka) A-bō-â-pri. Ta-bā-ôr-i pri-āx ar-ta-bas. A-dr(dir)-pan Cor-sta Do-bix. Yol-cam pri-ā-zi Ar-co-a-zior. Od quasb Q-ting. Ri-pīr pa-a-oxt Sa-gā-cor(kor). vm-L od prd(pur)-zar ca-crg(cōrg) Aoi-vē-â-e cor-mpt. Tor-Zu, Za-Car, od Zam-Ran aspt Sib-si But-mô-na ds Sur-zas Tia Bal-tan. Odo Cicle Q-ā-a, od oz-az-ma pla-pli lad-nâ-mad.

### Meditate with the Governors' Names

When you have finished reading the Enochian Call, repeat the names of the governors of the Aethyr you're working in out loud or silently (which I prefer). Start with the higher numbers first. Thus, if you're opening the Thirtieth Aethyr, you will pronounce the names of each of the four governors—beginning with the ninety-first governor (Dozinal), then the nineteeth (Advorpt), then the eighty-ninth (Gemnimb), and then the eighty-eight (Taoagla). All four of the governors belong to this Thirtieth Aethyr (all of the other Aethyrs have three governors). Close your eyes and use whatever method you feel most comfortable with. You can move from one angel to the next when you feel moved to do so. I usually dwell on the name of one governor for a few minutes or longer and then go to the next one for a few minutes. If you need to open your eyes to read the names of the governors in the book, that's fine. (Eventually, you will know them by heart and not have to refer to the book.)

Stay with one Aethyr for each session. For example, don't mix the governors of the Thirtieth Aethyr with those of the Twenty-ninth. Also, you don't have to use the governor's names as a continuous mantra. I like the example of going into a room and calling out the name of a friend. You keep calling him until he comes to you, and then you don't need to call his name anymore. When I feel the presence of a governor, I usually stop repeating his name.

However, if you want to keep repeating them, that's fine, too. I've done it that way and it's very effective. This is your personal meditation, and you need to experiment to see what's right for you.

## Names of the Ninety-one Governors of the Thirty Aethyrs

I have opted to *not* include the pronunciations of the governor's names on the CD that accompanies this book. This is because there is a little less definition as to exactly how they should be pronounced. Another reason is that it is better for people to arrive at the correct pronunciation themselves. If you are not pronouncing the angel's name correctly during your meditation, believe it or not, the angel will impress upon you the correct pronunciation. That's why I would rather leave this up to you.

**Note:** The straight line above the vowel is a long vowel: ā ē ī ō ū; the caret symbol above the vowel is a short vowel: â ê î ô û.

### 30. TEX

91. Do-zī-nal

90. Ad-vorpt

89. Gem-nimb (mmb)

88. Ta-ō-â-gla

### 29. RII

87. Gom-zī-am

86. O-drâx-ti

85. Vas-trim

### 28. BAG

84. Ox-lô-par

83. Fo-cīs-ni

82. Lab-nix-p

**27. ZAA**

81. Or-pâ-nib

80. Ma-thu-la

79. Sa-zī-â-mi

**26. DES**

78. Baz-chim (kim)

77. Ni-Grā-na

76. Po Phand

**25. UTI**

75. Ran-glam

74. Ob-uâ-ors

73. Mir-zind

**24. NIA**

72. So-ā-gê-el

71. Chi (Ki)-alps

70. Or-câ-mir

**23. TOR**

69. Zax-â-nin

68. O-ni-zīmp

67. Ro-nô-amb

**22. LIN**

66. Cal-zirg

65. Pa-rā-ô-an

64. O-zi-daī-a

**21. ASP**

63. Vix-palg

62. To-ān-tom

61. Chris-pa

**20. CHR (KAR)**

60. To-tô-can

59. Par-zî-ba

58. Zi-L-dron

**19. POP**

57. O-mâ-grap

56. Aba-ī-ond

55. Tor-zōx-i

**18. ZEN**

54. Yal-pa-MB

53. Za-fâ-sai

52. Na-ba-ô-mi

**17. TAN**

51. To-câr-zi

50. Ay-dropt

49. Sig-morf

**16. LEA**

48. So-chī (ki)-al

47. La-vâ-con

46. Cu-carpt

**15. OXO**

45. Tas-toxo

44. No-ci-â-bi

43. Ta-hân-do

**14. UTA**

42. O-ō-â-namb

41. Vi-uî-pos

40. Te-dô-and (Tedoond)

**13. ZIM**

39. Do-cê-pax

38. La-pâ-rin

37. Ge-cā-ond

**12. LOE**

36. Am-briol

35. Ge-dô-ons

34. Ta-pâ-mal

**11. ICH (ik)**

33. Po-nô-dol

32. Us-nār-da

31. Mol-pand

**10. ZAX**

30. Ta-bī-tom

29. Co-mâ-nan

28. Lex-ārph

**9. ZIP**

27. Do-ān-zin

26. Cral-pir

25. Od-dī-org

**8. ZID**

24. Pris-tac

23. Tod-na-on

22. Zām-fres

**7. DEO**

21. As-pī-â-on

20. Ge-nâ-dol

19. Ob-mâ-cas

**6. MAZ**

18. Zir-zird

17. Vā-vâ-amp

16. Sax-tomp

**5. LIT**

15. Ti-ār-pax

14. No-cā-mal

13. Laz-dix-i

**4. PAZ**

12. Poth-nir

11. Ax-zī-arg

10. Tho-tanf

**3. ZOM**

9. An-dīs-pi

8. Vi-rō-chi (ki)

7. Sa-mâ-pha

**2. ARN**

6. Di-a-lī-û-a

5. Pa-cās-na

4. Do-âg-nis

**I. LIL**

3. Val-gars

2. Pas-comb

I. Oc-cô-don

## 🌿 Part Three—Ending the Meditation

*When you're done repeating the names of the governors, take a few minutes to relax and come out of your deep rest.*

This is important since your body has been in a deep physiological state for fifteen to twenty minutes, and you need at least two or three minutes to readjust. Just stop thinking of the governor's names, and you will gradually come back to your normal state. You can also thank the spirits mentally for their help.

### Thank the Spirits (using your own words)

Thank the governors for appearing to you, spending time with you, and guiding you through their domain or Aethyr. You would do this for any friend who showed you around their town after a visit. I usually do this silently, but you can do it out loud if you prefer. Use your own words of thanks, whatever feels right to you.

*License to Depart (Read silently or out loud)*
O spirits (name the governors; here, for instance: Dozinal, Advorpt, Gemnimb, and Taoagla), because you have been very ready and willing to come at my call, I hereby license you to depart to your proper place. Go now in peace and be ready to come at my call when requested. May the peace of God be ever continued between you and me.

*Final Prayer*
You can make up your own prayer, thanking God or saying whatever you feel moved to say.

*Do the Closing Lesser Banishing Ritual of the Pentagram (Stand up and say it out loud)*
Sit down and rest for a few minutes before you get up and resume your activities.

## Recommendations for the Enochian Meditation

### Keep a Diary
Almost all magicians keep a diary, and I strongly suggest that you do too. After each session, write about your experiences, noting anything unusual or significant. This also allows you to chart your progress. (If Dr. Dee had not kept a diary you would not be reading this book!) You may discover something important for yourself or for others in the future. At the very least, you should record the date, the time, what Aethyr you've explored, and the results achieved. If you experienced any visual images or sounds during the meditation, record those as well. Believe me, you will forget everything very quickly, and it's important for you to have a record. (I used to use a digital recorder at the end of my sessions because sometimes so much happened I wouldn't get a chance to write it all down before I forgot it!)

### Go Slowly

Go slowly and enjoy the meditations. Don't try to analyze them while you're meditating. Just experience them—you can analyze them later on. It may take time to experience the Aethyrs in their fullest sense. But this makes sense. If you're exploring a new area or region, you're not going to see everything there is to see the very first time. You also need to adjust to the new environment and begin to use your new senses. Some people don't experience visual phenomena but may feel the presence of *something*. You may have different experiences in the same Aethyr at different times. Again, everyone is unique; enjoy this new adventure.

I would suggest that you stick with the procedure as I've outlined above for the first couple of weeks or longer. You can then modify it to suit your personal needs if you wish. Remember, magic is a science and an *art*. You're the artist, so tailor your meditation to suit your own personality.

### Conform the Meditation

If you're in a place where you need to be quiet, you can do the entire meditation in your mind, even the LBRP. After you have performed the LBRP for many months, you will start to develop the ability to do it silently. You will not have to stand up and physically make the pentagrams and move around to each of the four directions in order to complete it. Just sit with your eyes closed and visualize your movements and say the words silently to yourself. In fact, I find this method to be just as powerful as when I say them out loud, but this only happened after I did the exercise for some time—after its archetypal pattern has been established on the astral plane. It was after almost six months of doing the LBRP out loud that I was able to do it mentally with the same effect.

### Be Persistent

Israel Regardie, one of the most famous of the Golden Dawn magicians, said that persistence is the most important trait to have when practicing magic. So don't give up. As I've stated earlier, we all have different gifts and reach different levels at different times—don't compare yourself with others. You're a unique spiritual being. The Sufis say that there are as many paths to God as souls. God's Meditation is one of those paths, and I believe it is a very simple and effective one. There are also many variations you can do in this meditation so be unique and creative because you're the artist. The possibilities are infinite.

In the next chapter, I will answer some questions and concerns that may have come up for you during this meditation.

# 9

# EXPECTED RESULTS AND RECOMMENDATIONS

I originally was not planning on including this chapter, but as I was completing the book, I realized many people may have specific questions about the meditation after having tried it, so I will try to anticipate these questions.

## Questions and Comments

First, it's important to realize that every person is on their own unique spiritual path. As we process information through our physical and spiritual bodies, the information is clouded, colored, and altered by our personal makeup and experiences. We also have different abilities and talents, in both the physical and spiritual worlds. Some people may have the gift of seeing visual phenomena from the spiritual world; others may be able to hear sound; and others feel emotion. I'm not good at visualization so most of my experiences in the Aethyrs involve being aware of changes in my states of consciousness, subtle sensations, information and knowledge flowing in from a higher level, and a type of sensation which I call flavors.

Each Aethyr and each angel has a flavor of its own that I can identify; it's a repeatable phenomenon. For example, in our physical

138

world, we recognize someone or a specific place by the sight, sounds, smells of that person or place. This is its flavor. Whenever you encounter this place or person again, you immediately recognize it by its flavor. It's similar in the spiritual world but occurs on a higher spiritual level.

Another question that arises is: what if you feel uncomfortable during the process, or you feel negative energies? This has never happened to me, but my suggestion would be that if it happens to you, and if you're a Christian, say the name of Jesus three times. Many years ago, I was involved with some occult experimentation, and I felt a high level of negative energy coming at me. I had memorized the 101 names of God and repeated them. Nothing happened until I said the name of Jesus, and the negative energy went away. I was not a Christian at that time, but it made me realize that the name *Jesus* is so powerful that it helps no matter what your faith or belief may be.

I have to say that, since that time, I've developed a new understanding of the Cosmic Christ. If you follow a different belief system, use the name of a deity or a holy word appropriate to your beliefs and religion, and repeat it three times. Many times, in actual fact, there is no external negative energy; rather, it's being generated by our own minds and is of our own creation. These uncomfortable feelings may arise because the new sensations we're invoking are foreign to our everyday feelings and experiences. If this should happen to you, you now have an effective way of dealing with the situation.

It's possible that unusual physical phenomena may occur during or after your meditation. It's not a common thing, but it has happened to me on several occasions. It was not frightening but actually very inspiring and uplifting. Since you're involved with energies in the higher spiritual realm, they may affect some changes in the physical realm, which you have no control over. Again, this isn't anything to be concerned about. Maybe there is a lesson or message that the angels are trying to give you, and it may be one that's very enlightening.

One question that's often asked of me is: if we're entering the

Aethyrs and communicating with only the good angels, why do we need a License to Depart and a LBRP? That's an excellent question, and as I mentioned before and as far as I know, Dr. Dee and Kelley never used the LBRP or a License to Depart in *their* rituals. I use them for several reasons. It makes me feel that I'm on holy ground, and I want to be in this frame of mind when I undertake my Enochian Meditation.

The White Light Visualization is a technique that's also known to work for spiritual protection. As mentioned earlier, I use both it and the LBRP. You can use your judgment as to which to use, but I would at a minimum always use the LBRP before and after any Enochian Meditation or magical ritual. I like to also use the License to Depart as it acts as closure for the meditation. You're basically telling the angels that you're done with the session and they should leave and not interact with you anymore. It's also respectful to the angels because in a sense you're telling them goodbye for now, that until the next encounter, you will go back to your world and they to theirs.

If you don't experience results after you've tried the Enochian Meditation several times, wait a few days and try it again. Sometimes we're not ready—either mentally or spiritually—for certain techniques. I also must emphasize that you should not be under the influence of alcohol or drugs (except for prescription drugs) during this meditation. This meditation should be done with a clear mind.

I recommend that you do it alone in a room by yourself, someplace you will not be disturbed. If you're going to have a conversation with a close or intimate friend, you don't want to be disturbed—you want to be able to give that person your full attention. How much more so when our conversations are with angels and God? To avoid interruptions, I put a "Do Not Disturb" sign on my door, turn off my cell phone, and take my landline phone off the hook as well.

I don't know if anyone entering the room during a meditation that you're undergoing would be affected by your meditation. My feeling is that they probably wouldn't, but it would disturb *your* deep state of rest. In any event, I like to be safe and not expose anyone to any unnecessary energies they may not be prepared for. Again, we're not invoking evil angels, but we're experimenting with forces we don't have all the answers about.

What if there's an emergency and you have to stop in the middle of the meditation? Attend to the interruption, and when you come back, do the White Light Visualization or the LBRP and continue where you left off. (Of course, also repeat the LBRP when you close.) Remember, you're not surrounded by evil beings who want to harm you. You're doing something that's helping your spiritual development, with the assistance of good angels in their heavenly abode.

What I've been doing recently, if I'm interrupted and have to get up and go somewhere during the meditation, is visualize that the white light around me moves with me and continues to surround me no matter where I go. When I'm done taking care of whatever it is that I need to attend to, I go back to my chair and visualize the white light again and continue on where I left off.

I would not do this meditation too late at night since it energizes you and may keep you awake. Also, limit the time in which you meditate with the governors or angels to about fifteen minutes initially. You can increase this as time goes on and you become more comfortable with the process and also your individual reaction to it. I also like to be relaxed for a brief period of time before I do the Enochian Meditation.

It's interesting that, even in my dream state, if I'm experiencing negative forces or sensing negative energy, I can perform the entire LBRP ritual exactly as it should be done. Usually when dreaming our thoughts are fragmented and confusing, but this ritual is so deeply embedded in my mind or my astral body that I can do the entire ritual in my dream state if I need to.

In this book, I have only touched on one aspect of the Enochian Magic of Dr. Dee. The angels taught him other types of angelic magic, and you may want to learn about these also. (Again, I would refer you to Lon Milo DuQuette's book, *Enochian Vision Magick*.) When I first started practicing magic, I got a very clear message that "everything I do is a magical act." Our lives should be a constant magical invocation of our higher self, of the god within us. The only purpose of a magical ritual is to awaken this higher self within. If we ask our guides for help, I'm sure they will try to assist us. Every day, ask your spiritual guides and God himself to help and guide you in the right direction so you can ascend on your spiritual path toward cosmic consciousness. Listen to that soft voice within yourself. We must also learn to be patient. All things happen in their due time.

Secrecy is another rule of magic. Sometimes it's better to keep your experiences or revelations to yourself. When we share them, they may be misunderstood, and you may feel like you have thrown them to the dogs. Remember the biblical verse (Matthew 7:6), "don't cast your pearls before swine." I've experienced this many times. Often when I've had an incredible experience and have shared it with someone, it doesn't sound right—it doesn't come out the way I want it to. There are some things that are important to share, but you have to make this distinction and be selective. Share your new wisdom, knowledge, and experience with discretion. Sometimes, if you keep your revelations and insights within you, they simmer and become fuller!

At first you may not feel at home with this magical procedure. That's okay because over time you will adapt and feel more comfortable with it. In fact, I feel more aware and natural when I'm exploring the higher heavens than when I'm in the physical reality. They are both necessary for our spiritual learning, but the higher worlds always carry the higher reality.

This may not be necessary to say, but you should not believe and accept everything you read, even in this book. Be selective and evaluate everything. Take what is good and reject what isn't applicable to you. I've also discovered that some things that were bad for me years ago are now good for me. We're dynamic spiritual beings, and we grow and change over time. I like the expression, "You can never go home again." Once you start on the spiritual path, there is no looking back. The analogy of Lot's wife looking back and turning to a pillar of salt epitomizes this idea. Once we embark on the spiritual journey, we must keep going until we arrive at the source of the truth, which is God.

Life is a spiritual adventure.

I like the Quote in the *The Candle of Vision:*

Sitting in your chair you can travel further than ever Columbus travelled and to lordlier worlds than his eyes had rested on. Are you not tired of surfaces? Come with me and we will bathe in the fountain of youth. I can point you the way to El Dorado.[1]

You will begin to realize that the White Light Visualization and the LBRP, if done on a regular basis, build up residual power and protection and actually remain with you all day long. You don't lose protection when you leave the area where you practice magic. No one ever told me this, but I've experienced it after many, many months of performing these rituals on a daily basis. They always surround you and go with you throughout the day and are your constant companions.

Remember, magic is an art, and you're the artist.

Also, don't expect to receive all the answers. We have just begun our path, at least most of us have, and any revelations that we receive will take time and much effort. We're exploring unknown worlds and realms and have to figure out what to do as we go along. There's no instruction manual, although there are aids in the form of teachers, books, and spirit guides. We're the final judges. We have to decide who to listen to and what to accept.

Always test the spirits because we must be careful that we're not getting advice from a mischievous or evil spirit. That's why it's always important to use your knowledge and intuition when making a decision. Also, things that reflect love, kindness, charity, humility, and goodness are usually from God, but we must be careful. Too many people have gone wrong by thinking God or angels were speaking to them when it was really evil forces or mischievous beings. This isn't to scare you but to urge you to be careful and judge everything. We do this every day in our physical world, so why not do it in our spiritual world also?

Also, remember to always thank the angels for their guidance and insight as you would thank a friend who had helped you in some way. We should ask in humility and only want what is the will of God for us. If we're not meant to have a certain revelation, we should not push God or the angels for it.

Finally, we must not forget our relationship to others. We're all traversing the spiritual path together, and we depend on one another. Love and charity are the universal law. An angel once relayed to me that "we need to bring you up so you can bring others up." That was the first indication that one of my roles was to write a book to help others find God. But first I needed to do my part to learn and experience what I needed to, in order to teach others. I hope I've done that.

I also like to remember and follow these guidelines that I call my three golden rules of magic; they came to me during one of my rituals:

> Be humble in everything you do.
> God is in everything.
> God is in everybody.

The first guideline allows us to know our place in the spiritual realm and not to take things for granted. Also, realizing that God is in everything makes us walk on holy ground all day long. Finally, realizing that God is in everybody gives us charity and love for our neighbors and our fellow travelers on the path.

# Aleister Crowley

This book would not be complete unless I commented on Aleister Crowley, the English occultist and magician who was a member of the Golden Dawn and one of the founders of the OTO. Crowley attempted to enter all thirty Aethyrs and left a written record of his attempt. Crowley first tried to enter the Aethyrs in November of 1900 but didn't get very far. He only entered the Thirtieth and Twenty-ninth and stopped there; he felt they were overpowering. It's interesting that I also couldn't get past the Twenty-ninth Aethyr for many months. I also had the feeling of the overpowering presence of something very holy and thus held back. (Finally, my good friend, Lon Milo DuQuette encouraged me, so I pushed on.)

Crowley made another attempt in November 1909 in the area of the Sahara Desert with Victor Neuburg, an occult associate of his. He continued with the Twenty-eighth Aethyr and worked up to the First. He published his experience in his magazine, the *Equinox,* in 1911 under the title of "The Vision and the Voice" (this article was later published as a book). Crowley's visions are very bizarre to say the least, and he added much unnecessary ritual that Dee would never have approved of. In fact, to my mind, many of the rituals and practices that he used to supplement the Enochian Calls bordered on black magic. Much of Crowley's ritual was completely made up by him. It was unorthodox and would be repulsive to most people.

I *will* give him credit, though, for being one of the most gifted and talented magicians of all time—even though his life and practices were very controversial, and he was dubbed "The Wickedest Man in the World." Aleister Crowley may have come the closest of any one person to understanding the real significance of Enochian Magic. In Crowley's vision of the Twenty-second Aethyr, he describes a table of forty-nine characters. This is the same table that Dee generated from an early angelic communication in which the names of the angels of the seven planetary spheres were given.

146 Expected Results and Recommendations

When Crowley first saw this table appear, it was surrounded by numerous angels. There was light on the table, and he observed that it burned with an intolerable light that he had never observed in any of the other Aethyrs.[2] This is an interesting description of Crowley's experience in the Twenty-second Aethyr. I have to say that I also experienced one of the most profound altered states and the presence of God in the Twenty-second Aethyr; it was much deeper than any of the other Aethyrs I've explored.

Crowley's information makes sense in that the angels always stressed the importance of the number *seven* (seven angels), and the number *forty-nine* and its multiples. If Crowley's visions had not been so contaminated by his vivid imagination, perhaps the angels' revelations of the tables would have been more frequent and detailed. Perhaps previous information was blocked, and it may be that this was the only time the real message of the angels came through.

Crowley mentions that the light was extremely intense in the Twenty-second Aethyr. Perhaps it overwhelmed his imagination. Another way of looking at this is to imagine entering a room that you've never been in before, and it's filled with unique furniture and unusual décor. Instead of walking into this room and just observing what is there without bringing anything into it, what Crowley did when entering an Aethyr, in my opinion, was to bring in his own "stuff" and mix it with the other things in the room, leaving his visions clouded with his own preconceptions.

By analyzing Crowley's experiences in each of the Aethyrs and comparing them with our own and those of others, we may be able to see what was actually in the room and not generated from our own perceptions. When different people see and experience similar things in the same Aethyr, the objectivity and independence of that spiritual realm is revealed.

Another interesting difference between my technique and Crowley's is that, after Crowley recited the Enochian Call, he used a topaz to scry and to explore the Aethyrs. This is a method that many Enochian magicians use today. They employ a scrying stone (usually a crystal ball or black mirror) instead of closing their eyes and meditating like I do. I believe that my meditative technique is more natural than scrying and that more people will have success with it. I've experimented with scrying, with crystals and other objects, during my Enochian Meditation and have not had good results. (See plate 14 of the color insert, which is a photo of a crystal skull; crystal skulls can be used for scrying also.)

I know other Enochian magicians who scry using a black mirror or crystal ball, and they've had good results, but they seem to have an innate ability and talent for scrying. You can try both methods and see what works the best for you. Remember, your abilities are unique so try different things and go with what works for you.

I know from the diaries that Dee and Kelley used scrying to receive the tables and the Enochian Calls. However, there is no indication that once the Calls had been received, they continued to use the scrying technique. Just because this was the method of transmission for Dee and Kelley doesn't mean that this should be the preferred method today. Let me reiterate that I believe that meditation is the most natural and God-given way to communicate with God.

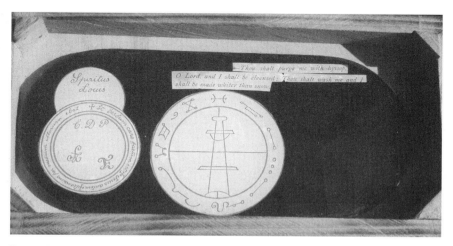

Figure 9.1. A black mirror made and used for scrying by Nick Nocerino, one of the world's foremost experts on crystal skulls.

Crowley also said that anyone with only the slightest capacity for magic will find that the Enochian Calls or Keys will work for them. I intentionally didn't read Crowley's book before I explored the Aethyrs since I didn't want my experiences to be influenced by his. Everyone should rely on their experiences and not those of others; thus, I don't recommend reading his book until you have explored the Aethyrs for yourself. And I can't overemphasize the importance of faithfully keeping a good spiritual diary.

I've already mentioned that initially Crowley had trouble getting past the Twenty-ninth Aethyr, and that I too had this same problem. It's important to realize that you may come to a limit in how far you can go as well. You may not be able to appreciate the higher Aethyrs beyond the particular level you're currently at. You need to follow your inner awareness regarding this. There is no need to race through all the Aethyrs; instead, go slowly and carefully. As mentioned, I spent many months on just the Thirtieth and Twenty-ninth Aethyrs before I advanced further. Everyone is different, and you need to determine your own pace.

Early this year, I began to realize that my task was to bring God's Meditation to the world, and I am thoroughly convinced that God and the angels want to share with everyone how to access the peace and presence of God. My sincere blessings to you—I wish you success on your spiritual path. May the Light of God illuminate all of you in your search and bring you to the final and only true reality, which is the presence of God.

# 10

# HIDDEN REVELATIONS OF ANGELIC MAGIC

It's so interesting how you can look at something 100 times and then the 101st time discover something you never saw before, and you can't believe you overlooked it. This happened to me with the Dee diaries. I was trying to put all the pieces of Dee's Enochian Magic into a completed puzzle, but something wasn't fitting properly.

## What Is the Real Function of the Tables?

The question that was nagging me is why did the angels go through all the trouble of creating the forty-eight tables letter by letter, a very time-consuming process, when they could have skipped this step and just given Kelley and Dee the forty-eight Calls directly letter by letter? Is it possible that the forty-eight tables themselves have another role or purpose?

In fact, and as I have discussed before, not all the Calls were generated from the forty-eight tables. It appears that the angels used the system of grid locations and giving the Calls in reverse order only for the first nineteen words of the First Call. Later they seemed to abandon this system—the Calls were given directly, letter by letter, and not in reverse order. With this method, the angel stood on a table and pointed to the letters on a turning globe or letters directly on a table. I know for certain that the Nineteenth Call, the one used to generate the thirty Calls, was dictated by the angel Illemes standing on a table that had a globe with letters on it. The globe would turn, and the angel would point to the letters on the globe that would form the Calls. The transmission of the Nineteenth Call began on Thursday, July 12, 1584:

> Dee: Now in the name of Jesus, as concerning those 30 Calls, or thirty Call, we await your information of Ilemese. . . .

> EK: Now he standeth as Nalvage used to do, upon the Globe with the rod in his hand: And Gabriel sitteth by. . . .

> Dee: In the name of the eternal and everlasting God say on.

> EK: Now the Globe turneth swiftly, and he pointeth to letters thus, with the rod which Nalvage was wont to use.[1]

This method of the angel pointing to letters on a globe is mentioned several times during the transmission of the Nineteenth Call. This call was transmitted during several angelic sessions. During one session, about halfway through the Call, the globe was mentioned again by Kelley:

> EK: Now they appear, and the Table, or Globe with them.[2]

The thirty Calls of the Aethyr generated by the Nineteenth Call were the most important part of Dee's Enochian Magic, but the tables were not even used for this. That's what bothered me, because the angels had made incredible statements about the forty-eight tables. After the Nineteenth Call is given, Gabriel makes the following statement about the tables:

Gabr. . . . . Thus hath God kept promise with you, and hath delivered you the keyes of his storehouses: wherein you shall find (if you enter wisely, humbly, and patiently) Treasures more worth than the frames of the heavens.[3]

From the time I began practicing Enochian Magic, I had not concerned myself with the tables. What would I use them for? What other functions might they have? This is where the missing pieces fall in. First, let's read what I found to be the most important sections in Dee's diaries concerning these tables.

On pages seventy-six and seventy-seven of Casaubon's 1659 edition of *A True and Faithful Relation of What Passed for Many Years Between Dr. John Dee and Some Spirits*, we have the following communications between the angel Nalvage, Dee, and Kelley, which took place on Thursday, April 12, 1584, while they were in Poland. The angel doesn't specify the time period, which this vision describes, but I think it's safe to say it can refer to many different times: times past, Dee's time, and most likely even our own. It's a timeless description of the world and of humanity:

The Godhead in his secret judgment keeping in his Almighty bosom, the image and form of all things, universally, looked down upon the Earth; for he said, Let's now go down among the sons of men: He saw that all things grew contrary to their creation and nature; either keeping their dignities and secret virtues shut up in obscurity, or else riotously perishing, through the imbecility and forwardnesse of ignorance: So that it was said, Behold, I delight not in the World: The Elements are defiled, the sons of men wicked, their bodies become dunghills, and the inward parts (the secret chambers of their hearts) the dens and dungeons of the damned: Therefore I will draw my spirit from amongst them, and they shall become more drunken, and their ignorance such as never was: No, not since the fall of the heavens.[4]

Nalvage is describing how bad and wicked human beings had become. Isn't this an apt description of the world today? Just look around. We're in ignorance of God and his will. He doesn't delight in the world. The "elements," nature and our environment, are defiled. Our atmosphere is polluted, and radioactive waste contaminates our planet. The secret virtues mentioned are our spiritual gifts, which people have ignored and buried. Instead of humans striving after God, we strive after material things and are filled with greed, selfishness, and lust. We keep our secret virtues shut up inside us; we don't use and expand upon our spiritual gifts.

A frightening allusion in the quote above is the comparison between today and the day of "the fall of the heavens." This is a probable reference to the time when a third of the angels rebelled against God and were cast out of heaven and fell to the earth, as described in the Book of Revelation and the apocryphal Book of Enoch:

> For, lo, the time is come, And he that's the Son of Unrighteousnesse, is and liveth: Unto him therefore shall be given strength and power: and the Kings of the Earth shall become mad: yea, even raging mad; yea even in the third madnesse, and that in the depth of their own imaginations; and I will build my Temple in the Woods, yea even in the Desert places; and I will become a Serpent in the wildernesses: for I've tucked up my garments and am fled away, and She shall mourn on the Mountains without comfort.[5]

The "Son of Unrighteousness" is the antichrist. We know this since Dee wrote "Antichrist" in the margin of his diary next to this name. What is interesting about this statement is that the angel says, "The antichrist liveth." Does that mean he is alive today and was alive in Dee's time? Maybe he has always been alive and is waiting for the end times to make his appearance. The "Woods" and "Desert places" (he capitalizes them) are our inner being where God dwells in our inner spiritual sanctuary.

Lo, the Thunder spake, and the earth became misty, and full of fogge, that the Soul of man might sleep in his own confusion. The second Thunder spake, and there arose spirits, such as are for Soothsayers, Witches, Charmers, and Seducers: and they are entered into the holy places, and have taken up their seats in man. Woe be unto the earth therefore: For, it's corrupted. Woe be unto the earth, for she is surrendered to her adversary: Woe be unto the earth, she is delivered into the hands of her enemy: Yea, Woe be unto the sons of men, for their vessels are poysoned. But even then said the Lord, Lo, I will be known in the wildernesse, and will Triumph in my weaknesse.[6]

Perhaps these "Thunders" are related to the seven thunders described in the Book of Revelation. The witches and charmers are, in my opinion, people who practice black magic and don't use magic for its true purpose of spiritual development and seeking God, as Agrippa and Dee wanted it to be used.

... it became a Doctrine, such was never from the beginning: Not painted, or carved: filed, or imagined by man, or according to their imaginations, which are of flesh: but simple, plain, full of strength, and the power of the holy Ghost: which Doctrine began, as man did, nakedly from the earth: but yet, the image of perfection. This selfsame Art is it, which is delivered unto you an infallible Doctrine, containing in it the waters, which runne through many Gates: even above the Gate of Innocency. . . .[7]

This "Doctrine," or the Book of Enoch (the tables) and the forty-eight Calls are not "painted or carved," meaning they are not just useless words or scripture but full of the power of the Holy Spirit and of God. They will open the doors to heavenly realms. The phrase "it's delivered unto you" and the use of the word *water* both symbolize spirituality.

The following is the most important message regarding the true purpose of tables:

> I'm therefore to instruct and inform you, according to your Doctrine delivered, which is contained in 49 Tables. In 49 voyces, or callings: which are the Natural Keyes, to open those, not 49, but 48 (for One isn't to be opened). Gates of understanding, whereby you shall have knowledge to move every Gate, and to call out as many as you please, or shall be thought necessary, which can very well, righteously, and wisely, open unto you the secrets of their Cities, and *make you understand perfectly that contained in the Tables.* Through which knowledge you shall easily be able to judge, not as the world doth, but perfectly of the world, and of all things contained within the Compasse of Nature, and of all things which are subject to an end.[8] (Italics mine.)

Thus, opening the gates by using the Calls and going into the cities (Aethrys) allows one to then unlock the forty-eight tables.

The forty-eight Calls allow us to enter the Aethyrs, and once inside, we're taught the secrets of how to read the tables as instructed by the angels. The angels had emphasized that the role of the tables is central, but this had just passed by me. I had been focusing on the Calls exclusively since the tables didn't seem to serve any additional purpose that I could figure out. But apparently one of the purposes of entering the Aethyrs (which the Calls allow us to do) is to unlock our understanding of the tables. I don't know how to do this, but maybe someone else does or will be able to figure it out in the future. (See the epilogue for my experiences with this.)

What's interesting is that in the diaries Dee specifically mentions that, when Kelley was in a trance, he was able to understand the tables. When the trance ended, he had no idea of their meaning. Maybe the trance mentioned is a reference to an altered state of consciousness like that produced with God's Meditation. I will share one of my experiences with regard to this as it may help others solve this puzzle.

# The Mysteries of the Twenty-second Aethyr

The following vision took place when I was exploring the Twenty-second Aethyr during my Enochian Meditation. (Remember that this was the same Aethyr in which Crowley received his vision and explanations of the table with the forty-nine squares of letters.) What's significant is that I usually don't get visual phenomena in my meditation, but this time I did. As I was meditating on the governors, I started to get into a very deep altered state, and I strongly felt the presence of God and the holiness of this Aethyr and his angels. The last governor seemed to open up my awareness of the purpose of the tables more completely.

I saw all of the forty-nine tables (not just the forty-eight) floating in space, and it appeared that each leaf was separated from the next one by about an inch. (Remember, the angels had deemed that the First Call and table was not to be shared with humans; that's why I think my vision is so extraordinary.) Then, the hand of God appeared, and his finger brushed or touched the first leaf, and it moved toward the second, and the second brushed the third, and so on and so forth. This was similar to dominos falling in slow motion. As each leaf hit the next one, something like letters or possibly notes came out from the leaves. They were numerous and floated majestically in the air.

A good way to visualize this is if you had forty-nine very dusty pages of a book. If you fanned the book, dust would fly into the air. In this case, it wasn't dust that came out but letters. They moved and floated in a beautiful harmony, almost like a symphony. I knew this symbolized the creation of the universe by God. His finger brushing the first leaf was like the OM Point or the Big Bang, which began everything. His finger was the Word of God (John 1:1). God only touched the first leaf, and as his hand moved or fanned over the rest of the leaves; the wind that he produced from the hand motion moved the rest of them in a domino effect.

This wind represents "The wind of God" mentioned in Genesis Chapter 1. Many bibles translate this section as "The spirit of God" but that is not correct. The wind was hovering over the deep before creation began. Some people translate the Hebrew word for wind as Holy Spirit. So, if this wind was the Holy Spirit of God, it was now taking over to finish the process of creating the universe. The English word *spirit* used here is translated from the Hebrew word *ruah,* which really should be translated as breath, wind. The religious people involved with the translation tried to imply it was the Holy Spirit but most scholars translate it as wind. In my vision, all three persons of the Godhead were present: the Father, the Son, and the Holy Spirit. Notice that God only touched the first leaf and no others. This is why the first leaf was never given to Dee, and he only received forty-eight and not forty-nine leaves. Since God actually touched the first one, it was too holy to be given to humans.

This vision is consistent not only with Christianity, in that the three aspects of God were present in the creation, but also Egyptian mythology. The Egyptian god Thoth was considered the tongue of God, through which the will of God was translated into speech. He has also been compared to the Logos or the mind of God. In addition, he was the Egyptian god of magic and writing. He was considered to be the scribe of the gods and was credited with inventing the alphabet.

The letters coming out of the pages would be consistent with a cosmology where Thoth ruled as a god. He was the god who originated all things; the Egyptians believed that he was responsible for making all of the calculations for the establishment of the universe, including the stars, the planets, the earth, and everything they contained. It's very interesting that his female counterpart Maat controlled the movement of all things in the universe and was the force which maintained creation—in other words, the wind.

In Crowley's vision of the Twenty-second Aethyr, an angel plays a pipe, and according to Crowley, the music is wonderful. The angel stops playing and moves his fingers in the air, which leaves a trail of fire of many colors. There is some similarity between this and my vision of God moving his finger in the air and fanning the forty-nine tables.

Crowley also seemed to see visions of the creation and dissolution of the universe. In my vision, I only beheld the creation. (Keep in mind I didn't read Crowley's description before I explored the Twenty-second Aethyr.) I was very grateful to the angels for revealing the vision of the Twenty-second Aethyr to me. It was one of the most sublime revelations I have ever received in my exploration of the Aethyrs.

In conclusion, it would appear that the tables are the final key to unlocking the secrets of God. Are we meant to do this during this time of human existence, or will the secrets be unlocked at some time in the future? That's another question I cannot answer.

## A Few Last Thoughts

The Angel Gabriel made the following interesting statement:

> Thus hath God kept promise with you, and hath delivered you the keys of his storehouses: wherein you shall find (if you enter wisely, humbly, and patiently) Treasures more worth than the frames of the heavens. . . . Therefore, now examine your Books, Confer one place with another, and learn to be perfect for the practice and entrance. See that your garments be clean.[9]

You must be prepared spiritually: as the angel says, "enter wisely, humbly, and patiently." How many magicians take the time to be in the proper state of body and mind before they practice their ritual magic? Are their lives consistent with these characteristics? Do they approach magic with humility and reverence? The phrase "See that your garments be clean," is a metaphor for spiritual cleanliness. Remember that Agrippa pointed out that one's frame of mind and attitude is of the utmost importance in magic.

I want to leave you with an idea that came to me during one of my recent Enochian Meditations. I was asking one of the angels to help me understand the tables, and the angel said to me, "What do the Tables contain that was not used in generating the forty-eight Calls?" I took out my copy of the tables from the British Library and realized almost immediately that over each table (of the forty-nine by forty-nine grid pattern) was a title in the Enochian language (the meaning of which we have no idea). These titles were not used in generating the forty-eight Calls. Perhaps these titles are a key to something that's waiting to be discovered.

In this book, I have attempted to show that magic is a spiritual practice that helps one to experience God's presence and the higher realms or heavens that are within all of us. Magic is a spiritual path in our ascent or way back to God. The purpose of our existence is for us to become God-conscious, that is, to attain cosmic consciousness. I believe the practice of magic is the simplest and most direct method or means to attain this goal. Both Henry Cornelius Agrippa and Dr. John Dee believed this, and that was their sole purpose in studying and practicing magic. Magic opens up the spiritual world and hence the spiritual path for seekers of God. We attempt, through our practice of magic, to move closer and closer to God as we traverse the higher realms of the heavens.

So, if we sincerely believe the above and are using the practice of magic and magical meditations for spiritual development, then who or what are we?

## We Are Mystics!

Mystics are individuals who transcend normal consciousness and are awakened to a higher reality. They experience the direct presence of God and his attributes. The veil is torn, and they now have spiritual vision and understanding. They now know the secrets of nature and feel the oneness of God within them. This experience is one that they never forget, and it can never be put into words, as hard as they may try to. This transcendence brings the true awareness and presence of God—his love, peace, and harmony. It is an infinite blissful or ecstatic state, which reveals everything and the purpose of everything.

This spiritual illumination is the goal of life. The greatest mystics have tried to write about this experience, and they have given us glimpses. (See the writings of St. John of the Cross and St. Teresa of Avila.) This experience or state is dormant within every person and is just waiting to express itself. The attainment of this state is the birthright of every individual.

Thus, magic, as I see it, is a mystical path toward God, and we are the mystics on that path.

I would like to conclude this book by reflecting on the words *occult* and *esotericism*. The word *occult* means hidden or secret knowledge. *Esotericism* or *esoteric knowledge* has a similar meaning and refers to knowledge given or revealed to only a select few. I believe times have changed, and now this occult knowledge, of which Enochian Magic is a major part, is to be revealed to the masses and not just to the select few. That's the purpose of this book.

If what the angels say about these tables is true, we're sitting on one of the most important discoveries in the history of humankind: the knowledge and understanding of all things in the universe, the highest mysteries of God that a person can know. It's just waiting to be discovered by someone. The angels made these statements about the tables:

Wherein, they will open the mysteries of their creation, as far as shall be necessary: and give you understanding of many thousand secrets, wherein you're yet but children; for every Table hath his key: every key openeth his gate, and every gate being opened, giveth knowledge of himself of entrance, and of the mysteries of those things whereof he is an inclosure.[10]

One is one: neyther is, was or shall be known: And yet there are just so many. These haue so many names, of the so many Mysteries, that went before. . . . O what is man, that's worthy to know these Secrets?[11]

This boke, and holy key, which unlocketh the secrets of god his determination, as concerning the begynning, present being, and ende of this world, is so reuerent and holy: that I wonder (I speak in your sense) whie it is deliuered to those, that shall decay: So excellent and great are the Mysteries therein conteyned, aboue the capacitie of man. . . . One thing excepted: which is the use thereof. Unto the which the lord hath appointed a day.[12]

The angels told Dr. Dee not to read this book aloud or try to understand it until the appointed time:

God shall make clere when it pleaseth him: & open all the secrets of wsidome whan he unlocketh. Therfore Seke not to know the mysteries of this boke, tyll the very howre that he shall call thee.[13]

Perhaps that time is now?

# FINAL DISCOVERIES ABOUT THE TABLES OF ENOCH

As I was coming to the end of writing this book, some important information was revealed to me. Given its significance, I've opted to include it here.

## The Key to Reading the Tables of Enoch

My first discovery regarding reading the tables of Enoch occurred when I was exploring the Twenty-second Aethyr in my Enochian Meditation. (As you will recall, this was an important Aethyr for both Aleister Crowley and myself.) I was told by the angel of that Aethyr that the key to the tables is in the first leaf—the one composed of paragraphs of Enochian words, which were supposed to fit into the forty-nine by forty-nine grid patterns.

In the first two tables (unlike the rest—see appendix A) an entire Enochian word would be placed in the cell instead of a single letter, so Kelley had to write out the words in a long string (they would not fit into the small cell area). The angel told me that the ninety-four tables should also be read as a string of Enochian words. That is, start with row one, column one and list all the letters together until the end of that row, at that point there should be forty-nine letters. Continue with the next row, until all the 2,401 letters are written out, one after another. I was told to do this for each table.

I asked, "How will I know how to separate the words since it would be just a string of letters?" He said, "When you look at the tables it will be apparent." I had no idea what he meant. So, I started looking at a scan of the tables on my computer and enlarged them so I could read each letter; that was not easy as the tables are very messy and the handwriting difficult to discern. As I was attempting to write down each letter in each cell, I noticed small commas and sometimes periods between groups of letters. I assume that's what the angel was referring to when he said, "It will be apparent."

I was totally surprised because I've studied these tables numerous times and never noticed the very small commas or periods. After I wrote out a few lines and separated the letters using commas to create words, I tried to read them. It's interesting that the words *did* sound like the Enochian language. Unfortunately, not all the tables have these commas and periods so there may be other clues with regard to how to separate the characters into words. I'm in the process of investigating this further.

If you will recall, another hint I received was that at the top of each table is a title in the Enochian language, which of course no one has been able to interpret. I had been told that these were an important key in that they were *not* used in producing the Calls. Maybe they tie in somehow with the string of letters forming the words. I am continuing to investigate this also, and my search has led me to my next revelation.

## The Missing Tables of Dr. Dee

I propose that we may have an original table in Dee's handwriting. The full set of tables that we have today is written in Kelley's hand, but we don't know for certain if Dee wrote the initial set and then Kelley copied it later, leaving the recopied set for posterity.

We *do* know, as I've stated earlier in this book, that the tables were transmitted to Kelley by an angel pointing to a letter on his table. Kelley would see what that letter was and then repeat it out loud. Now, we don't know if Kelley wrote the letters down on his set of tables as he saw them, or if Dee wrote them down on his set after Kelley repeated them out loud. I believe Dee wrote them down because what reason would Kelley have to repeat them unless someone was listening to copy them, and that person would have to have been Dee?

What evidence do we have for this? We do know that *MS 3189* (the ninety-four tables with the several pages of Enochian words at the beginning) are all in Kelley's handwriting. Thus, if Dee initially wrote them down, Kelley must have later made a copy from Dee's original. We have to ask if there are additional tables in Dee's handwriting, and the answer is yes. In the preface of Meric Casaubon's *A True and Faithful Relation of What Passed for Many Years Between Dr. John Dee and Some Spirits,* Casaubon stated that at the back of these diaries there were many tables. He went on to say that he would only reproduce one of them as it would be too costly to reproduce all of them. In addition, he didn't think they were very significant.

The table in the 1659 book can be compared with the identical one in *MS 3189* that's in Kelley's handwriting. I discovered that the one in Casaubon's book is in Dee's handwriting, not Kelley's. (I'm able to distinguish between Dee's and Kelley's handwriting by the way they formed some of their letters in a distinct way.) I realize it was redrawn by the engraver of the plate, but he must have traced or followed Dee's characteristic handwriting and the way he formed his letters. (Obviously, he must have used Dee's original drawing of this table.)

Thus, I believe that the tables in the back of Dee's spiritual diaries that Casaubon was referring to were the *original* ones drawn by Dee all in Dee's handwriting. Aside from a copy of this one table, the rest are all missing or destroyed. We only have the one that Casaubon decided to reprint in his book. There also is a discrepancy between the table in the Casaubon book and the same table in *MS 3189*; there appears to be

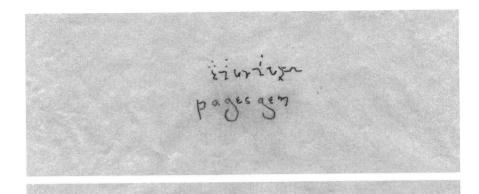

Figure E.1. The top script is from *MS 3189* in Kelley's handwriting with the shortened title. The bottom script is from the sample table in Casaubon's book—it's one of the missing Dee tables and is a representation of Dee's handwriting. (Redrawn by the author.)

more information on the Dee table, and the title of the table is longer in that it has additional Enochian words.

Did Kelley abbreviate and leave things out when he copied Dee's original tables? Is the *MS 3189* Kelley copy that we currently have in the British Library not a true and complete copy? Is there anything missing that would affect the supernatural effects or properties of these tables? Remember, I was told that the titles are a key to all of this. We will not know unless we eventually recover the missing Dee tables, which I believe are in Dee's handwriting and are the original or first ones drawn and, in fact, may contain additional information that was not included in the Kelley copies of the table.

# The Discovery of the First Table

As I discussed in chapter 7, there are in reality forty-nine tables, but only forty-eight were given to Dee and Kelley. The first table was never given since the angels said that the soul of a human has no portion in this table and that this table neither is, was, or shall be known. I believe at a later date, the angels changed their mind, and Dee was given the first table. I may have discovered and deciphered it from Dee's notes and diaries.

Figure E.2. The front side of the first leaf reconstructed

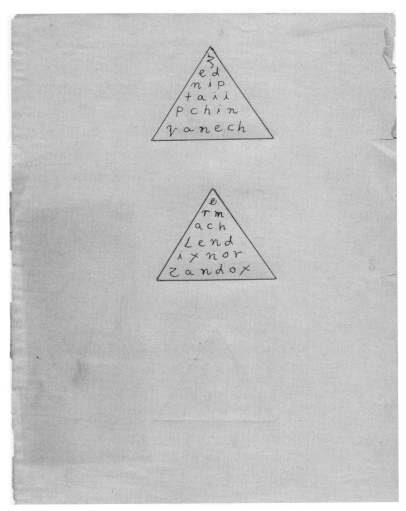

Figure E.3. The back side of the first leaf reconstructed

I tried to reconstruct it according to the directions Dee was given by the angels and have included mention of it in this book because it's possible someone else may discover its meaning or shed some light on it. It's a mystery to me why the angels at first told Dee and Kelley they would not give them this table and then apparently changed their minds. I also want to verify that I've identified and interpreted this information correctly. I will give all the details of this in a follow-up book to be published by Inner Traditions. In this forthcoming publication, the complete Book of Enoch will be reprinted for the first time.

If you have made any discoveries, I would enjoy hearing from you so I can include this information in my next publication for others to take advantage of. I can be reached by e-mail at drjohn@gizapyramid. com. Or you can reach me through the website that I've created for this purpose: www.myangelmagic.com. I believe we can only solve these enigmas if we all work together. Even the Bible says, "For where two or three are gathered in my name, I AM there among them" (Matthew 18:20).

I believe we're all on this spiritual path together, and by helping each other, we will make more rapid progress to our ultimate goal of cosmic consciousness.

# APPENDICES

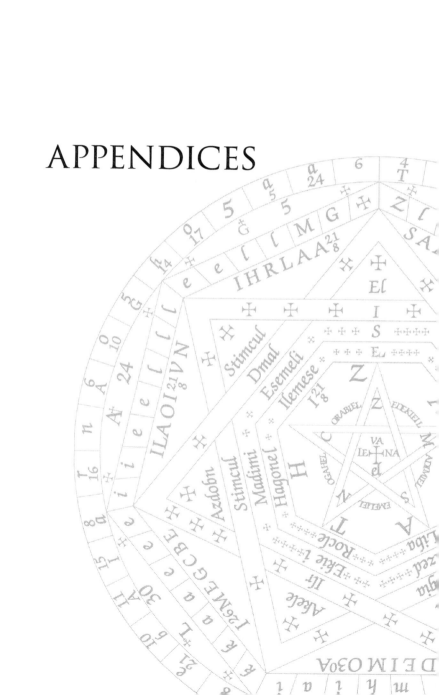

# Appendix A
# THE QUESTION OF
# THE TABLES

Let's now turn our attention to the tables. I've been referring to them as ninety-five in number. The originals are in the British Library, and there are definitely ninety-five of them there. But here's what's confusing: the angels refer to these tables as the set of "forty-nine Tables." So why the discrepancy?

I believe the answer lies in a statement made by an angel. The angel "Ile," who later delivered the Calls to Kelley, said that

Every Table containing one whole leaf. . . .[1]

Book collectors know that one leaf is composed of a front and a back. So, one leaf would contain two tables, one on the front side of the paper and one on the back side (referred to as the verso). For simplicity's sake, let's assume there were actually ninety-four tables instead of ninety-five. (We will see later why this assumption is justified.) If we divide ninety-four by two, we get forty-seven.

The angels had also said that the First Call couldn't be given to them as it's too heavenly or spiritual to be given to humans. Dee and Kelley were given forty-eight tables, not forty-nine. We're still short one table.

To confirm that only forty-eight tables were transmitted to Kelley and Dee, let's read the angels' own words and the actual vision of the book that Kelley observed on March 24, 1583. Notice that the angel uses the word *leaves* and not *pages* (remember, there are two pages per leaf). The angel also makes it clear that there are forty-eight total leaves.

First, Kelley observes that the angel Medicina Dei is holding a book. This is the Book of Enoch. The angel says:

> All the LEAVES are like gold and it seems that they were written with blood, not dried. . . . There are 48 LEAVES [Capitals are my emphasis, and I've modernized the English].

Then the angel "Medicina Dei" says:

> One . . . shall not be known.[2]

This definitely states that the Book of Enoch (which the angel was holding) has forty-eight leaves, and they are leaves and not pages. Kelley and Dee will not be shown the first leaf so they will only have the forty-eight to use.

Let's look in detail at this book that is in the British Library (known as *Sloane 3189*) and which Dee called the *The Liber Loagaeth*. The entire book itself consists of:

- Eight pages of Enochian words; we have no idea what they mean.
- One page with a table of nine lines composed of forty-nine letters per line.
- Ninety-five pages of individual tables.
- Finally, one blank page and one page with the twenty-one characters of the Enochian alphabet.

These first eight pages of Enochian words are in groups of—let's call them paragraphs. There are forty groups or paragraphs, and each paragraph is composed of forty-nine separate Enochian words. Each word is supposed to fit into one space of a forty-nine by forty-nine table (instead of one letter). Since Kelley couldn't fit these words into the allotted space, he wrote it out in a long sentence. Thus, the forty-nine words in paragraph one would fill in the forty-nine columns in row one.

Paragraph two also has forty-nine Enochian words, which fit into each column on row two, and so forth. So, when we get done with the forty paragraphs of forty-nine words each, we have forty of the forty-nine rows filed in. Now, on the last page, is a table of nine rows by forty-nine columns, each one of which is filled in with a letter. These additional nine rows complete the table of forty-nine rows and forty-nine columns. So, these eight pages and the nine by forty-nine table make up one complete table. This is identified as the back side of the first leaf. The first side of the leaf isn't in this Book of Enoch but in another manuscript (*MS 3188*). Kelley never copied the first side of the first leaf into the Book of Enoch (*MS 3189*). In *MS 3188,* there are forty-nine groups or paragraphs of forty-nine Enochian words, so each word fits into one of the spaces in the forty-nine by forty-nine table. So, we now have two tables, one on the front side of the first leaf and the other on the back side of the first leaf. Thus, we have the first of the forty-eight leaves with two tables, one on the front and one on the back.

Thus, ninety-four tables plus the two additional tables, which are made up of the pages of Enochian words in each cell, equals ninety-six pages of tables. If we divide it by two, we get forty-eight *leaves.* This is consistent with the angels' statement that there are forty-eight tables or leaves.

Remember, there are actually ninety-five pages of tables in the British Library copy, and I assumed for our calculations there were only ninety-four.

I went through the British Museum scans in detail, and lo and behold, I found a page that was reproduced twice. Whoever did these scans many years ago must have thought that the first scan of this page was too light, so they scanned it again but didn't discard the extra scan. That's my opinion of what probably happened. So, if you eliminate the duplicate page, you now actually wind up with ninety-four tables! (If you want to verify this, the duplicate page is numbered 18 in the manuscript in the British Library.)

# Appendix B

# THE ENOCHIAN MEDITATION SUMMARIZED

After you have performed this meditation many times, have learned it well, and have memorized the LBRP, you won't need to read over all the explanations and discussions in chapter 8. This page is a summary to have in front of you when you do the meditation:

## ENOCHIAN MEDITATION SUMMARY

### Preparation

- Sit near a lighted candle

  *Meditate on how the candle connects you with the Light of God and the Presence of God.*

- White Light Visualization (read the following):

  *May the white light surround me.*

  *May the white light elevate me and put me in touch with my spiritual guides.*

  *May the white light connect me with the Divine Light, the Light of God.*

- Do the Lesser Banishing Ritual of the Pentagram (LBRP)

  *First you will first do the Kabbalistic Cross, and then you will construct the Pentagram of White Light.*

**The Kabbalistic Cross**

- Stand facing east.
- Visualize the Light of God coming to you and hovering over your head in a dazzling ball of light.
- Reach up with your right index finger and bring this ball to your forehead and touch your forehead.
- Say or chant: AH-TEH (Unto Thee . . .).
- Move straight down and touch your chest or stomach and say or chant: MAL-KUTH (. . . the Kingdom . . .). (As you move your finger to each part of your body, visualize the white Light of God moving with you, and at the end, you will have a large cross over your body from the white light.)
- Touch your right shoulder and say or chant: VEE-GE-BUR-AH (. . . and the Power . . .).
- Touch your left shoulder and say or chant: VEE-GE DU-LAH (. . . and the Glory . . .).
- Finally, bring your hands together in front of you like in prayer and say or chant: LE-OL-LAM (. . . Forever . . .).
  *AH-MEN.*

**The Pentagram of White Light**

- Facing east, trace a large pentagram in the air. (As illustrated in figure B.I on page 174, start at the lower left side of the pentagram and move in the directions indicated.)
- When the pentagram is complete, thrust your right index finger in the center of the pentagram and say or chant: YOD-A-HAY, VAV-A-HAY.
- Turn and face south.
- Make the same pentagram in the air (starting at the lower left side), and when completed, thrust your right index finger in the center and say or chant: AH-DO-NAI.

Figure B.1. Start at the lower left corner and trace the pentagram in the direction indicated until you come back to the starting point.

- Turn to the west, trace the pentagram, and, when completed, say or chant: E-HI-YAY.
- Turn to the north, trace the pentagram, and when completed, thrust your right index finger in the center and say: AH-GA-LA.
- Turn to the east and thrust your finger in the center of the pentagram you traced initially, thus completing a closed circle of four pentagrams. Visualize this circle and the pentagrams as a vibrant light surrounding and protecting you.
- Still facing east, stretch out your arms in the form of a cross and chant the following:
  *Before me: RA-FAY-EL.*
  *Behind me: GA-BRE-EL.*
  *On my right: ME-CHI-ALE.*
  *On my left: UR-REE-ALE.*
- Keep your arms outstretched and continue by saying:
  *Before me, flames the pentagram.*
  *Behind me, shines the six-rayed star.*

- Repeat the Kabbalistic Cross once more, and you're now done with the LBRP.

## The Enochian Call
## (The Call of the Thirty Aethyrs)

Mā -drî -iax Ds praf (Name of Aethyr, i.e., TEX) ch(k)īs Mi-cā-olz Sa-ā-nir Ca- ōs-go, od fī-sis Bal-zi-zras Ia(ya)-ī-da, Non-ca(sa) Go-hū-lim, Mic(Mīk)-ma A-do-ī-an Mad, I-ā-od Bli-ōrb, Sâ-ba-o-o-ā-ô-na ch(k)īs Lu-cīf-ti-as pe-rīp-sol, ds Ab-ra-ās-sa Non-cf(sf) Ne-tā-â-ib Ca-os-gi od Ti-lb Ad-phaht Dām-ploz, To-ō-at Non-cf(sf) Gmi-cāl-zô-ma L-rāsd Tōf-glo Marb yār-ry I-doi-go od Tor-zulp ia(ya)-ō-daf Go-hōl, Ca-ōs-ga Ta-ba-ord Sa-ā-nir od Chris-tê-os Yr-pō-il Ti-ō-bl, Bus-dir ti-lb No-aln pa-id ors-ba od Dod-rm(rum)-ni Zyl-na. El-zāp-tilb Parm-gi pe-rīp-sax, od ta Q(K)urlst Bo-o-a-pi-S. Lnib(Lmb)-m o-v-cho Symp, od Chris-tê-os Ag-tol-torn Mirc Q Ti-ōb-l Lel. Ton pa-ombd Dil-zmo As-pī-an, od Chris-tê-os Ag L tōr-torn pa-rāch A-symp, Cord-ziz Dod-pal od Fi-falz Ls-mnad, od Farg-t Bams O-ma-ō-as. Co-nīs-bra od A-uâ-vox To-nug, Ors-cāt-bl No-âs-mi Tab-gēs Levith-mong, un-chi(ki) Omp-tilb Ors. Bagel. Mo-ō-ô-ah ol cōrd-ziz. L ca-pī-mâ-o Ix-o-māx-ip od ca-cō-casb Go-sâ-a. Ba-glen pi-i Ti-ān-ta A-bā-bâ-lond, od fa-ōrgt Te-lōc-vo-vim. Mā-drî-iax Tor-zu O-ād-riax Or-ō-cha(ka) A-bō-â-pri. Ta-bā-ôr-i pri-āx ar-ta-bas. A-dr(dir)-pan Cor-sta Do-bix. Yol-cam pri-ā-zi Ar-co-a-zior. Od quasb Q-ting. Ri-pīr pa-a-oxt Sa-gā-cor(kor). vm-L od prd(pur)-zar ca-crg(cōrg) Aoi-vē-â-e cor-mpt. Tor-Zu, Za-Car, od Zam-Ran aspt Sib-si But-mô-na ds Sur-zas Tia Bal-tan. Odo Cicle Q-ā-a, od oz-az-ma pla-pli Iad-nâ-mad.

## Meditate with the Governors' Names

See list of names on pages 130–34.

## End the Meditation

- Thank the Spirits
- Intone the License to Depart

  *O spirits, because you have been very ready and willing to come at my call, I hereby license you to depart to your proper place. Go now in peace and be ready to come at my call when requested. May the peace of God be ever continued between you and me.*

- Do the Closing Lesser Banishing Ritual of the Pentagram

# Appendix C
# JESUS AND THE ANGELS

I was debating whether or not to add this section to the book since I did not want to give the impression that I was trying to push my personal views or beliefs on anyone. I hope by now, after reading this far, you realize that I do not believe in evangelizing or trying to convince any-one of my personal beliefs. We all need to find God for ourselves and within ourselves using our own means. Forcing your beliefs on someone else does not work. In fact, it has the opposite effect.

When I was director of religious education I saw this many times at different churches. It seemed that if a religious belief had been forced on a child, as soon as they became an adult and left home, they aban-doned their faith and stopped going to church. This is most likely the case with almost anything in life. If you try to force your viewpoints or beliefs on anyone, they will most likely reject them as soon as they have the opportunity, even if what you tell them is the truth. I have tried to emphasize throughout this book that finding God is a personal and intimate experience. My approach and the one I have suggested is to find God through meditation. I believe that this is the most natural and gentle way to experience him.

After reading the final draft of this book, I realized I may have left out an important aspect of this angelic communication, which most authors choose to ignore. I felt that to leave this out would be to do an injustice to the message of the angels. What I am specifically referring to are statements made by the angels about the role and importance of Jesus Christ. Thus, putting my own beliefs aside, I feel it is important to cover this ground in an objective way.

We know from Dee's diaries and writings that he was a devoted believer in Jesus Christ as the Son of God. But what did the angels say about this, and how is it relevant to what we have been discussing? Some may argue that the statements made by the angels were consistent with Dee's beliefs and practices and were expressed in such a way as to make them acceptable and consistent with his views. However, this does not make sense; the angels said many other things that were contrary to Dee's beliefs and religious views.

Let's look at some of the statements made by the angels that are about Jesus. I have selected what I believe are some of the most revealing ones:

Madini: I rejoyce in the name of Jesus, and I am a poor little Maiden, Madini. . . .[1]

Gabriel: For behold, you participate (in) the mercies of God through his Son Christ Jesus, in that we open unto you those things that have been sealed. . . .[2]

Gabriel: Charity is the gift of the Holy Ghost, which Holy Ghost is a kindling fire, knitting things together, through Christ Jesus; in the true wisdom of the Father. . . . For it is the meat of us that are anointed, which is the son of God, and the light of the world.[3]

Dic illis: My name is called Dic illis. I am one under Gabriel, and the name of Jesus I know and honour.[4]

Uriel: Is not Jesus, God, and the High Priest of the Lord placed on the right hand of his Father?[5]

An angel: O you of little understanding: Who is he that can and hath to give, but God, Jesus Christ the Sonne of the living God, unto whom all things are given in Heaven, and in Earth. . . .[6]

An angel: Now then if you be man, then are you of earth, earthy. But according to your similitude, grafted in the image of God in his Sonne Jesus you are heavenly.[7]

An angel: For he that dwelleth in Christ is quick, because he dwelleth in life and light. But he that goeth out of Christ through sin, and in whom Christ dwelleth not, he is dead.[8]

Raphael: In the Name of Jesus Christ, I Raphael am now sent unto you to deliver unto you your question so far forth as God his will and pleasure is to command me. . . .[9]

Raphael: In the Name of him that created me Raphael, and all the blessed Creatures, and likewise in his power made all the world, and all things therein contained: Jesus Christ of his great goodness hath sent me now at his will, and so I am bound at his will to return, when his pleasure is. All honour be given to him being God Almighty for evermore. Amen.[10]

So, to summarize the main points of the above quotes, the following are the attributes and the role of Jesus:

- Angels rejoice in the name of Jesus.
- Jesus opens up mysteries that have been sealed for us. (Compare Revelation.)
- The true wisdom of the Father can be found in Jesus.
- Jesus is the light of the world.
- The angels know and honor the name of Jesus.
- Jesus is placed on the right hand of the Father.

- All things, both in the heavens and on the earth, are given to Jesus.
- We are grafted in the image of Jesus, the son of God.
- Those that dwell in Jesus are alive and of the light.
- Jesus has sent Raphael to Dr. Dee to communicate this angelic communication.
- Jesus is God Almighty.

It is apparent from the above quotes that the angels believed Jesus is the Son of God: he was given all power in heaven and earth; his name is very powerful; and he has sent his angels to communicate important spiritual truths to Dr. Dee.

The name of Jesus is the most powerful name to use to protect yourself spiritually. I shared a story earlier in the book in which the name of Jesus protected me from negative influences when the other hundred names of God had no effect. This is very significant to me and something important for me to share with others.

Because of my experience with this, I add the name of Jesus to my opening prayer for the Enochian Meditation and also include his name in the License to Depart. This really gives me added comfort, and I feel very much protected with his presence.

Do I believe Jesus is the Son of God? How important is this belief? I cannot judge others or comment on their beliefs, but this is an important tenet of mine. I do not believe in Jesus in the way traditional and evangelical religions believe in him. I view Jesus more as a cosmic Christ that is in everyone and is the personal aspect of God that we can connect with. I believe Jesus is the sum total of the attributes of God that incarnated in human beings. When some say Jesus is the Son of God, we really have no idea what that means. It is just a way of trying to visualize or understand a spiritual mystery. I remember a statement made back in the 1970s by a follower of Meher Baba, a highly respected spiritual teacher from India. In fact, I was a follower of Meher Baba for many years and feel his simple philosophy helped me start to look for

God within myself, without being shackled with religious beliefs and ideology.

Even though today I do not accept everything Meher Baba taught, he was a powerful influence in my life. One of Meher Baba's well-known followers was asked if he believed Meher Baba was an avatar or God-conscious person, and his response was that the concept and understanding of what an avatar is goes beyond his comprehension and spiritual wisdom. It would be like asking a child to understand the Theory of Relativity. I feel the same way about Jesus. I do not have the spiritual wisdom to determine if he is the Son of God, but I do believe that he is the most important spiritual teacher that ever lived and embodied what I believe are the attributes of God. If that makes me a Christian, so be it, but I do not like labels. I feel the best description of Jesus is that he is the embodiment of the attributes of God incarnate and was born and died in order to give light and guidance to human beings.

One aspect of Jesus which many Christians do not always emphasize is the comfort that he brings. When I meditate or need some help, I withdraw into the presence of Jesus. It is similar to my approach when I meditate with the presence of God, but if I use Jesus' name, something more personal is communicated. It's difficult to capture in words, but the feelings evoked are ones of warmth, protection, love, and peace. It is not really much different than what I feel when I'm with God; it's perhaps another way to experience God.

I think other spiritual teachers throughout history have shared some of God's attributes and that is why many people were attracted to them and followed their teachings. However, I don't believe any of them came close to fully embodying the attributes that Jesus had. He truly embodied the concept of God for us in human form.

Jesus is important in my life for these reasons, which may or may not be shared by most Christians. I try to keep my beliefs simple and nourished by my meditation. To make my point clear and not give a false impression, I want to end with my favorite Sufi saying, one that

I have quoted earlier: "There are as many paths to God as souls in the world."

**Author's Note:** After I wrote this appendix, I decided to meditate on whether or not to include this section in the book since I didn't want to alienate any readers who don't believe Jesus has a special significance in the greater scheme of things. I was deliberating over which Aethyr to enter when I strongly felt the angels calling me back to the Twenty-second Aethyr, which, as I have previously mentioned, was one of the most powerful Aethyrs that I have explored. It was the one in which I experienced a very intense presence and the Light of God. Also, as discussed in chapter 9, this was one of the most intense Aethyrs that Aleister Crowley experienced.

After the Lesser Banishing Ritual of the Pentagram and the White Light Visualization, I decided to open my Bible to a random place and read what was there. (I usually do not do this.) When I did this, it opened on the first chapter of John. This was very appropriate, because I was asking whether or not to include a section on what the angels said about Jesus:

> In the beginning was the Word, and the Word was with God, and the Word was God. The same was in the beginning with God. All things were made by him; and without him was not anything made that was made. In him was life; and the life was the light of men. And the light shineth in darkness; and the darkness comprehended it not.
>
> JOHN 1:1 (AV)

The angels told me that even today we have not comprehended who Jesus really is and what he is. All the religions have additional doctrines created by humans that have distorted the true meaning of Jesus. Maybe the angels are also trying to restore that meaning today, and that's why they mentioned and discussed Jesus so much throughout their spiritual communications with Dee.

I was told to pick up my pencil and write. This was an unusual request during my Enochian Meditation. This is what I wrote:

> God is the greatest thing (or concept) that man could comprehend in the world. No other concept should be considered. Meditate on God all day long. Jesus is the extension of God for human understanding and relationship. Do to others what you would do to Jesus. Love. Love. Love. Harmony. Harmony. Harmony. This is the original concept of Creation.

Their response to my question to the angels regarding whether or not to include this appendix to the book was, "Yes, yes, yes! This crowns the book!" Then they said, "No other questions please. Meditate and relax!"

After this I experienced the most incredible peace of God pervading everything. I felt lighted up like a Christmas tree and felt that the angels were smiling at me!

The final words I received from the angels were:

> The Light of Jesus will purify, cleanse, and elevate you.
> Man's job is to meditate on God. God's job is to elevate man.
> We cannot elevate ourselves on our own without the help of God.

Remember the saying, as we take one step toward God, he takes ten steps toward us.

# NOTES

### Foreword

1. DuQuette, *The Chicken Qabalah of Rabbi Lamed Ben Clifford,* 202.

### Chapter 1.
### Magic and Its Influence on
### Our Everyday Lives

1. Agrippa, *Three Books of Occult Philosophy,* 3.

### Chapter 3.
### Magic in Ancient Civilizations

1. King, *Babylonian magic and sorcery,* 115.
2. Budge, *Egyptian Magic,* 3–4.
3. Spence, *An Encyclopedia of Occultism,* 135.

### Chapter 4.
### The Renaissance Magician—
### Henry Cornelius Agrippa

1. Agrippa, *Three Books of Occult Philosophy,* 554.
2. Ibid., 2.
3. Ibid., 346.

## Chapter 5.
## He Spoke to Angels—
## The Life of Dr. John Dee

1. Dee, *To the Kings most excellent Maiestie*, 1.
2. Dee, *A letter, containing a most briefe discourse apologeticall*, B3.
3. Letter from Albert Einstein to Herman E. Peisach, February 15, 1946.

## Chapter 6.
## The Angelic Magic of Dr. Dee

1. Casaubon, *A True and Faithful Relation of What Passed for Many Years Between Dr. John Dee and Some Spirits*, 174.
2. Ibid., 62.
3. Ibid., 3.
4. Ibid., 9.
5. Ibid., 10.
6. Ibid., 73.
7. Ibid., 237.

## Chapter 7.
## The Transmission of the
## Enochian Tables and the Forty-eight Calls

1. Casaubon, *A True and Faithful Relation of What Passed for Many Years Between Dr. John Dee and Some Spirits*, 64–65.
2. *Sloane 3188*, f101b.
3. Peterson, *John Dee's Five Books of Mystery*, 300–303.
4. Casaubon, *A True and Faithful Relation of What Passed for Many Years Between Dr. John Dee and Some Spirits*, 79.
5. Ibid., 73.
6. Ibid., 82–83.
7. Ibid., 87.
8. Ibid., 101.
9. Ibid., 78.
10. Ibid., 209.

11. Ibid., 145.

12. Ibid., 88.

13. Ibid., 78.

14. Ibid., 79.

15. Ibid., 141.

16. Ibid., 139–40.

## Chapter 8.
## How to Practice the Enochian
## Meditation—A Practical Guide

1. Personal communication, 2009.

## Chapter 9.
## Expected Results and Recommendations

1. Russell, *The Candle of Vision*, 55.

2. Crowley, *The Vision & the Voice with Commentary and Other Papers*, 78.

## Chapter 10.
## Hidden Revelations of Angelic Magic

1. Casaubon, *A True and Faithful Relation of What Passed for Many Years Between Dr. John Dee and Some Spirits*, 200–201.

2. Ibid., 206.

3. Ibid., 209.

4. Ibid., 76.

5. Ibid., 76–77.

6. Ibid., 77.

7. Ibid.

8. Ibid.

9. Ibid., 209.

10. Ibid., 88.

11. Peterson, *John Dee's Five Books of Mystery*, 263.

12. Ibid., 393–94.

13. Ibid., 351.

## Appendix A.
## The Question of the Tables

1. Casaubon, *A True and Faithful Relation of What Passed for Many Years Between Dr. John Dee and Some Spirits,* 199.
2. *Sloane 3188*; and Peterson, *John Dee's Five Books of Mystery,* 263.

## Appendix C.
## Jesus and the Angels

1. Casaubon, *A True and Faithful Relation of What Passed for Many Years Between Dr. John Dee and Some Spirits,* 1.
2. Ibid., 37.
3. Ibid., 40.
4. Ibid., 145.
5. Ibid., 232.
6. Ibid., 361.
7. Ibid., 367.
8. Ibid., 372.
9. Ibid., *37.
10. Ibid., *39.

# BIBLIOGRAPHY

Agrippa, Henry Cornelius. *De incertitudine et vanitate scientiarum et artium, atque excellentia verbi Dei declamation* [*The Vanity of Arts and Sciences*]. Paris, 1531.

————. *De Occulta Philosophia.* Antwerp, 1531.

————. *De Occulta Philosophia Libri Tres.* Cologne, 1533.

————. *Three Books of Occult Philosophy.* London, 1651.

————. *The Fourth Book of Occult Philosophy.* London, 1655.

Budge, E. A. Wallis. *Egyptian Magic.* London: Kegan, Paul, Trench and Trübner & Co., 1901.

Casaubon, Meric. *A True and Faithful Relation of What Passed for Many Years Between Dr. John Dee and Some Spirits.* London: D. Maxwell, 1659. (Reprinted by Askin Press, London, 1974.)

*Chronological Study Bible.* Nashville, Tenn.: Thomas Nelson, 2008.

Clark, Andrew. *Aubrey's Brief Lives—chiefly of Contemporaries, set down by John Aubrey, between the years 1699 and 1699.* London, 1898.

Crowley, Aleister. *The Vision & the Voice with Commentary and Other Papers.* York Beach, Maine: Samuel Weiser, 1998.

Deacon, Richard. *John Dee: Scientist, Geographer, Astrologer, and Secret Agent to Elizabeth I.* London: Frederick Muller, 1968.

Dee, John. *General and Rare Memorials Pertaining to the Perfect Art of Navigation.* London, 1577.

————. *A letter, containing a most briefe discourse apologeticall with a plaine demonstration, and feruent protestation, for the lawfull, sincere, very faithfull and*

*Christian course, of the philosophicall studies and exercises, of a certaine studious gentleman: an ancient seruant to her most excellent Maiesty royall.* 1599.

———. *To the Kings most excellent Maiestie.* London: E. Short, 1604.

———. *The Hieroglyphic Monad.* London: John M. Watkins, 1947.

Debus, Allen G., ed. *John Dee, The Mathematicall Praeface to the Elements of Geometrie of Euclid of Megara (1570).* New York: Science History Publications, 1975.

DeSalvo, John. *Dead Sea Scrolls: Their History and Myths Revealed.* Barnes and Noble, 2009.

DuQuette, Lon Milo. *Enochian Vision Magick: An Introduction and Practical Guide to the Magick of Dr. John Dee and Edward Kelley.* San Francisco, Calif.: Weiser Books, 2008.

DuQuette, Lon Milo. *The Chicken Qabalah of Rabbi Lamed Ben Clifford: A Dilettante's Guide to What You Do and Don't Need to Know to Become a Qabalist.* York Beach, Maine: Weiser Books, 2001.

Einstein, Albert. Albert Einstein to Herman E. Peisach, February 15, 1946. http://dowsingworks.com/einstein.html. Accessed March 11, 2010.

Fenton, Edward. *The Diaries of John Dee.* United Kingdom: Day Books, 1998.

French, Peter. *John Dee: The World of an Elizabethan Magus.* New York: Dorset Press, 1972.

Hislop, Alexander. *The Two Babylons.* Neptune, N.J.: Loizeaux Brothers, 1916.

James I, King of England. *Daemonologie in forme of a dialogue, diuided into three bookes.* Edinburgh: Robert Walde-graue Printer, 1597.

James, Geoffrey. *The Enochian Magick of Dr. John Dee.* St. Paul, Minn.: Llewellyn, 1994.

Kaiser, Jr., Walter C. and Duanne Garrett, eds. *Archaeological Study Bible: An Illustrated Walk Through Biblical History and Culture,* New International Version. Grand Rapids, Mich.: Zondervan, 2005.

King, Leonard W. *Babylonian magic and sorcery: being "The prayers of the lifting of the hand," the cuneiform texts of a group of Babylonian and Assyrian incantations and magical formulae edited with transliterations, translations and full vocabulary from tablets of the Kuyunjik collections preserved in the British Museum.* London: Luzac and Co., 1896.

Laycock, Donald C. *The Complete Enochian Dictionary.* San Francisco, Calif.: Weiser Books, 2001.

Manuscripts from the British Library. Sloane 3188, 3189, 3191; Cotton Appendix XLVI. *Parts 1 and 2.*

Morley, Henry. *Cornelius Agrippa: The Life of Henry Cornelius Agrippa von Nettesheim, Doctor and Knight, Commonly known as a Magician.* 2 vols. London: Chapman and Hall, 1856.

Nauert, Charles G., Jr. *Agrippa and the Crisis of Renaissance Thought.* Urbana: University of Illinois, 1965.

Peterson, Joseph H. *John Dee's Five Books of Mystery.* San Francisco, Calif.: Weiser Books, 2003.

Raphael. *The Familiar Astrologer.* London: T. Noble, 1849.

Regardie, Israel. *The Golden Dawn.* St. Paul, Minn.: Llewellyn, 1971.

Russell, George William. *The Candle of Vision.* London: Macmillian and Co., 1918.

Russell, Walter. *The Universal One.* New York: Brieger Press, 1926.

Shumaker, Wayne, ed. and trans. *John Dee on Astronomy—Propaedeumata Aphoristica (1558 & 1568).* Berkeley: University of California Press, 1978.

Skinner, Stephen and David Rankine. *Practical Angel Magic of Dr. John Dee's Enochian Tables.* London: Golden Hoard Press, 2004.

Smith, Charlotte Fell. *John Dee (1527–1608).* London: Constable and Co., 1909.

Spence, Lewis. *An Encyclopedia of Occultism.* New York: Dodd, Mead, and Co., 1920.

Suster, Gerald. *John Dee, Essential Readings.* Great Britain: Crucible, 1986.

*The Holy Bible, English Standard Version (ESV).* Wheaton, Ill.: Crossway Bibles, 2001.

Turner, Robert. *The Heptarchia Mystica of John Dee.* Great Britain: The Aquarian Press, 1986.

———. *Elizabethan Magic.* Great Britain: Element Books Limited, 1989.

Tyson, Donald. *Three Books of Occult Philosophy.* St. Paul, Minn.: Llewellyn, 1993.

———. *Enochian Magic for Beginners.* St. Paul, Minn.: Llewellyn, 2007.

Vinci, Leo. *An Enochian Dictionary GMICALZOMA.* England: Authors OnLine Ltd., 2006.

# ABOUT THE AUTHOR

John DeSalvo, Ph.D., is director of the Great Pyramid of Giza Research Association. His purpose in starting this association was to make available to the public general information and new research on the Great Pyramid and to post the work of pyramid researchers who may not have had the opportunity to publish their work in the traditional academic journals.

A former college professor and administrator, his B.S. degree is in physics, and his M.A. and Ph.D. degrees are in biophysics. He has taught the following subjects on the college level: human anatomy and physiology, biochemistry, general biology, human gross anatomy, and neurophysiology. His college administrative experience includes cultural affairs director, basic science department head, and dean of student affairs.

In 1979 DeSalvo coauthored of the book *Human Anatomy—A Study Guide* (currently out of print) with Dr. Stanley Stolpe, former head of the Anatomy Department at the University of Illinois. His publications in scientific journals include research on the infrared system of rattlesnakes ("Spatial Properties of Primary Infrared Neurons in Crotalidae"). He was also a recipient of research grants and fellowships from the National Science Foundation, United States Public Health and Human Services, and the National Institutes of Health.

For more than twenty years, John DeSalvo was one of the scientists involved in studying the Shroud of Turin. Currently, he is executive vice-president of ASSIST (Association of Scientists and Scholars International for the Shroud of Turin), which is the largest and oldest research association in the world currently studying the Shroud of Turin. He was also a research consultant to the original STURP (Shroud of Turin Research Project) team and was the contributing science editor for the book *SINDON—A Layman's Guide to the Shroud of Turin* (published in 1982, currently out of print). His Shroud research involved the image formation process of the man on the Shroud and studies using three-dimensional reconstruction, spectroscopic, and ultraviolet analysis. He has lectured nationwide on the Shroud, and in 1980 the International Platform Association designated him as one of the top thirty speakers in the nation.

He published *The Complete Pyramid Sourcebook* in 2003 and *Andrew Jackson Davis: The First American Prophet and Clairvoyant* in 2005. His book *Decoding the Pyramids* was published by Barnes and Noble in May 2008 and has been translated into French, Spanish, Italian, Dutch, and Czech.

In October 2008, his book *The Seeress of Prevorst: Her Secret Language and Prophecies from the Spirit World* was published by Inner Traditions. His most recent book, *Dead Sea Scrolls,* was published by Barnes and Noble in July 2009 and is also available in French, Dutch, Spanish, and German.

# INDEX

# BOOKS OF RELATED INTEREST

**Enochian Magic and the Higher Worlds**
Beyond the Realm of the Angels
*by John DeSalvo, Ph.D.*

**Decoding the Enochian Secrets**
God's Most Holy Book to Mankind as Received by
Dr. John Dee from Angelic Messengers
*The Original Text with Commentary by John DeSalvo, Ph.D.*

**John Dee and the Empire of Angels**
Enochian Magick and the Occult Roots of the Modern World
*by Jason Louv*

**Dictionary of Ancient Magic Words and Spells**
From Abraxas to Zoar
*by Claude Lecouteux*

**Occult Botany**
Sédir's Concise Guide to Magical Plants
*by Paul Sédir*
*Translated with commentary by R. Bailey*

**Introduction to Magic**
Rituals and Practical Techniques for the Magus
*by Julius Evola and the UR Group*

**The Morning of the Magicians**
Secret Societies, Conspiracies, and Vanished Civilizations
*by Louis Pauwels and Jacques Bergier*

**Original Magic**
The Rituals and Initiations of the Persian Magi
*by Stephen E. Flowers, Ph.D.*

Inner Traditions • Bear & Company
P.O. Box 388
Rochester, VT  05767
1-800-246-8648
www.InnerTraditions.com

Or contact your local bookseller

# USING THE ENOCHIAN MEDITATION CD

The purpose of this CD is to review some of the key procedures of the Enochian Meditation that I discuss in the book and for you to hear how the words of the basic Enochian Meditation (otherwise known as the Call of the Thirty Aethyrs) should be pronounced so that you can learn and use its correct pronunciations for your own meditation practice. The CD contains the following:

Track 1 is an overview of basic suggestions for the entire Enochian Meditation.

After this general overview, we begin our preparation for the meditation itself. Proper preparation includes performing both the White Light Visualization and the Lesser Banishing Ritual of the Pentagram. Instruction and commentary on the White Light Visualization is found on track 2, and commentary and pronunciations of the Lesser Banishing Ritual of the Pentagram are on track 3.

We then enter the heart of the meditation itself, wherein I will pronounce the entire Enochian Call (otherwise known as the Call of the Thirty Aethyrs) on track 4.

The next part of the CD will focus on meditating on the names of the angels or governors of each realm. Track 5 contains commentary on this process.

The closing steps to take to end the Enochian Mediation are found on Track 6.

Track 7 contains final comments and suggestions for you as you learn to integrate this practice into your life.

I wish you the best of luck in your Enochian Meditation!